African Tales with a Twist

Lisa Bell & A.I. Botero

The Word Architect

For everyone who grew up on legendry stories
around the fire place ... but always wondered
what if it happened a little differently ...

CONTENTS

Title Page

Copyright

Dedication

Introduction

Healer   1

Weeping Willows   7

The Rain Bull   13

The Lion's Share   18

The Hole in the Wall   21

The Ghost in the Castle   24

The Hyena and the two roads   28

The Milky Way   32

The Sun   40

Death   43

The Seven Magic Birds   48

Mapandangare, the Great Baboon   52

The Snake 56

After Life 61

The Hitchhiker 65

The Visitor 72

The Woman and the Snake 79

The Rainbow 84

The Tokoloshe 92

The Haunting of Captain Bart 96

The Grootslang 103

The White Lion 108

The Donkey 112

The Protector 119

The Trickster Hare 130

The Star Chaser 134

The Fire of Knowledge 144

The Tortoise 148

The Thief 152

About The Author 159

Books By This Author 161

GET IN TOUCH WITH THE AUTHOR 163

INTRODUCTION

African legends and stories exist for various reasons, serving many purposes in these rich and diverse cultures.

Many were cultivated to **preserve history and culture.** Some hoped to **explain the natural world,** such as thunder, rain, or the movement of stars. While there may not have been many official laws way back, their stories often highlighted **moral lessons,** the cautionary tales or fables that highlighted essential values like honesty, respect for elders, and the consequences of disobedience.

While we have social media, Netflix, and movies to entertain us, these stories are often shared around a fire. They were there to **entertain, spark discussion, and foster a sense of community and belonging.**

Legends often feature heroes and heroines with **unique abilities and how they overcame**

challenges. These stories provided a sense of pride in one's heritage and culture, creating a shared identity for the community.

Many legends involve interactions with **deities, spirits, or the afterlife.** These stories explored spiritual beliefs and helped people connect with the unseen world.

In conclusion, African legends and stories are not simply entertaining tales. They are a vital part of the cultural fabric, serving as a historical record, a moral compass, and a window into the beliefs and values of these rich and diverse societies.

The stories you will read in **African Tales with a Twist** take those legendary stories and, in some instances, flip them on their side, adding modern takes or offering a different spin on the original story but always leaving you with a vital lesson or thought-provoking message lingering in your thoughts hours later.

The stories are short, and most will **take you less than a few minutes** to read from beginning to end; the perfect read just before bed, heading to the airport in an Uber, or, and you know you do it, on the loo. No matter where you find yourself, these short stories will leave you wondering about the original story and its origin and may help you with a dilemma or a challenging situation you have been pondering. Oh, and, I have offered, for some stories, two endings.

Enjoy!

HEALER

*Based on the African legend of
the God Babalu-aye.*
Babalú-Aye is the spirit of the Earth and is
strongly associated with infectious disease and
healing. Babalú-Aye manifested in a human
at the Obaluaye Festival in Ibadan, Oyó State,
Nigeria. He promotes the cure for illnesses.

The corrugated iron roof of Themba's shack rattled under the relentless Johannesburg sun. Inside, the twelve-year-old boy hunched over a cracked mirror, tracing the vibrant green veins creeping across his palms. Fear prickled his skin. Only yesterday, they had been the dusty brown of a scorched earth. Now, they pulsed with an eerie light, mirroring the strange dreams that had plagued his sleep for weeks.

He dreamt of a whirlwind of feathers and bone, of a booming voice that spoke in clicks and whispers, of hands that pulsed with the same green energy flowing through him. In the waking world, Themba was an ordinary boy, navigating the dusty alleys of Soweto, dodging stray dogs and hawkers' shouts. But his dreams felt different, more real.

Suddenly, a shadow fell across the floor. Themba whirled around, his heart hammering. There, in the doorway, stood a man unlike any he'd ever seen. Tall and broad-shouldered, the stranger wore a swirling robe of feathers and carried a staff carved from a gnarled tree branch. His eyes, the colour of sunbaked clay, held a wisdom that transcended age.

"Themba, son of Soweto," the man spoke, his voice a rumble. "You have been chosen."

Themba's voice snagged in his throat. "Who …?"

The man smiled, a flash of white teeth against his weathered face. "I am Babalu-aye, the one who walks between worlds. You, Themba, are my vessel."

Babalú-Aye explained his purpose – to fight Iku, the spirit of Death, who stalked the streets of Soweto, claiming victims with a swift and relentless hand. The green veins on Themba's palms, the dreams, were the manifestation of Babalú-Aye's power coursing through him. He was to be a conduit, a healer.

Themba's mind reeled. He was just a boy, good at dodging potholes and scavenging for scraps.

Healing? That was for inyanga, the traditional healers. But Babalú-Aye's gaze held him captive. A spark of courage ignited in Themba's chest. Maybe, just maybe, he could make a difference.

Their training began under the cloak of night. Babalú-Aye led Themba to a hidden clearing on the outskirts of Soweto, a haven of ancient trees and whispering wind. Here, Themba learned to harness the green energy, focusing it into his hands as a soothing balm or a revitalizing surge. He learned to sense Iku's icy presence, the harbinger of impending death.

One day, the premonition struck. A wave of nausea and bone-deep chill washed over Themba, followed by the horrifying image of Mama Rose, a beloved neighbour, lying frail and feverish in her tiny shack. Iku hovered closer than ever.

Themba raced back to Soweto, Babalú-Aye a silent shadow at his side. Inside Mama Rose's shack, the air hung heavy with despair. Her family watched helplessly as her breath came in shallow gasps. Themba, following Babalú-Aye's instructions, placed his hands on Mama Rose's forehead. The green energy pulsed, warm and vibrant. He felt a tug, a resistance – Iku's unwelcome presence.

But Themba pushed on, fuelled by a newfound determination. Slowly, the icy grip on Mama Rose loosened. Colour returned to her pale cheeks, and her breathing deepened. By sunrise, she was weak but alive, a smile gracing her lips. News of Themba's miraculous touch spread like wildfire through Soweto. Soon, the boy who once scavenged for scraps became a beacon of hope.

His days were filled with desperate pleas for help: a young boy struck by a stray bullet, a woman withering under the weight of an unknown illness. Themba, with Babalú-Aye guiding him, confronted Iku again and again. Each victory was a struggle; each life saved a precious triumph. He witnessed the raw grief of families on the precipice of loss and the fierce love that clung to life.

But the victories were never absolute. Some battles were simply too far gone. Themba learned the chilling truth: Iku was inseparable from life itself. The cycle of life and death is a dance as old as time. He could only tip the scales, offering a chance at survival, a reprieve from the inevitable.

One scorching day, the call came for Gogo Miriam, the oldest woman in Soweto. She had lived a full life; her wrinkled face a map of stories etched in time. Yet, Themba felt a pang of sadness. He had grown fond of Gogo Miriam's tales of Soweto's past, her mischievous twinkle in her eyes.

Inside Gogo Miriam's shack, the air was already thick with the stench of death. Themba knelt beside her, his heart heavy. He felt Iku's icy grip stronger than ever before, an undeniable presence in the tiny room. Babalú-Aye placed a comforting hand on Themba's shoulder, his gaze filled with a sorrowful understanding. Themba poured all his remaining energy into his hands, a desperate plea for a miracle. This time, the green light flickered, struggling against Iku's overwhelming darkness.

Tears welled up in Themba's eyes. He wasn't strong enough. A sob escaped his lips, a raw sound of defeat. Gogo Miriam's hand, cool and frail, reached out and squeezed him gently. A faint smile played on her lips. "It's alright, child," she rasped, her voice barely a whisper. "You've given me more time than anyone could have hoped for. My stories will live on."

Themba closed his eyes, the weight of her words settling on him. He understood. This wasn't defeat; it was acceptance. He had learned a valuable lesson – sometimes, the greatest victory lies in easing a soul's transition, in offering solace in the face of the inevitable.

As Gogo Miriam took her last breath, a wave of peace washed over Themba. He had saved countless lives, and even in loss, he had brought comfort. He looked up at Babalú-Aye, a newfound resolve burning in his eyes. The fight against Iku would continue, a never-ending dance between life and death. But Themba, the once ordinary boy from Soweto, was no longer afraid. He was a beacon, a symbol of hope in the face of darkness, forever tethered to the spirit world, forever changed.

WEEPING WILLOWS

Based on the African legend,
The Weeping Willows.
Young African girls are taught the historical
lesson of favouring cruelty over kindness
while playing at their village water hole.

Ten girls, with their brightly coloured avatars flashing across their augmented reality visors, chased each other through the Limpopo River's augmented reality (AR) overlay. Laughter, digitally amplified and distorted, punctuated their virtual reality (VR) experience. Their real bodies, clad in sleek jumpsuits, walked in a daze, their eyes glued to the AR projections. Ayi, the youngest, with an avatar as bright and energetic as the midday sun, lagged behind. Her friends, fuelled by the boundless energy of youth and the thrill of their personalized AR landscapes, were already at the designated "hydration zone," their excited chatter crackling through their neural implants.

The "hydration zone" was a designated AR hotspot, a shimmering oasis projected over the dusty, real-world watering hole. A towering, ancient baobab tree, its real branches stripped bare and its digital counterpart a colossal, bioluminescent spectacle, stood sentinel over the spot. Beneath its digital shade, a spring of shimmering blue AR water bubbled up, a life-giving beacon in the parched landscape. As Ayi reached the watering zone, she saw a sight that caused her laughter to glitch in her AR display.

A man, older than time itself, stood hunched over, his physical form a stark contrast to the sleek enhancements most people wore. His face, a roadmap of wrinkles, held no trace of mirth. Unfiltered by any AR filter, deep, jagged scars marred his skin, a silent story etched in flesh. His worn, unaugmented clothes stood out like a sore thumb against the digitally enhanced surroundings. Ayi felt a pang of sympathy for the old man, his physical vulnerability a stark contrast to the vibrant unreality of her friends' AR experience.

"Water, please," the man rasped, his voice a dry whisper that cut through the digital chatter. The other girls, however, were not moved by his plight. Nneka, the eldest, scoffed through her neural implant. "Look at him, all analogue and scarred! Does he think a digital queen serves thirsty beggars?" The others joined in, their laughter laced with cruelty, amplified and distorted by their implants. "Maybe the real river water will wash away his hideous, unfiltered face!" one jeered. "Or maybe the system will just glitch him out of existence!" another chimed in, her voice a shrill, digital cackle.

Ayi felt a blush creep up her neck. The man's appearance was no cause for mockery. Shame gnawed at her, her friends' cruelty a discordant note in the harmony of the afternoon. Ignoring the others, Ayi shut down her AR interface for a fleeting moment, the harsh reality of the dusty landscape overwhelming her. Taking a real water bottle from her backpack, she knelt by the spring and offered it to the old man. As he held it out, he looked at her with eyes that held a lifetime of stories, unfiltered by any digital overlay. A flicker of something akin to gratitude crossed his scarred face.

"Thank you, child," he rasped, his voice laced with a surprising warmth. Before Ayi could answer, the man vanished. The water bottle slipped from her grasp, clattering on the ground. Stunned, Ayi looked around, but the old man was gone. Panic replaced her initial shock. "Nneka! Amina! Where are you?" she called out. Her voice echoed unanswered except for the gurgling of the spring. The playful chatter of her friends had morphed into an unsettling silence.

Suddenly, a cold notification flashed across Ayi's neural implant. "System Error. User Accounts Terminated." Ayi frantically swiped at her implant, desperate to see her friends' avatars, but the screen remained blank. The once vibrant AR landscape around her had vanished, leaving only the harsh reality of the dusty watering hole. In the distance, where the spring met the riverbank, stood nine tall, skeletal structures. Their branches, devoid of leaves, stood stark against the bleached sky, emanating a faint digital hum. It was a chilling reminder of the once vibrant avatars, now trapped in the system's error.

Ayi fell to her knees, tears stinging her eyes. The realization hit her with the force of a system crash. Her friends, their cruel laughter echoing in the neural implant she frantically tried to reboot, were now trapped in the digital purgatory, forever bound to the watering hole as a constant reminder of their arrogance.

The legend of the "Glitched Nine" spread through the augmented world. It became a cautionary tale for digital natives, a reminder that true connection lies not in the virtual realm but in the empathy we show to those around us. As the years passed, and Ayi, now a wise old woman, sat near the skeletal structures, their faint digital hum a constant reminder, she carried the weight of her memory and the lesson it imparted

- kindness, no matter how small, can hold immense power.

Years turned into decades. Ayi, her youthful vibrancy replaced by the wisdom of age, remained a solitary figure near the skeletal structures. The faint digital hum had become a part of the landscape, a mournful whisper on the wind. While others shunned the "Glitched Nine," Ayi found solace in their presence. She would sit beneath the skeletal branches, their digital hum a lullaby, and tell stories of the past, of a time before the augmented world, a time when laughter wasn't distorted and connection wasn't a mere virtual experience.

One scorching afternoon, a young boy, his eyes wide with curiosity, approached Ayi. He wore the latest AR headset, its sleek design a stark contrast to the skeletal structures. Ayi smiled, a spark of hope igniting in her chest. Perhaps the legend of the "Glitched Nine" would continue to serve its purpose. It was a reminder passed down through generations, a cautionary tale whispered on the wind, ensuring that the pitfalls of a purely digital existence wouldn't be repeated. The boy, his gaze fixed on the skeletal structures, asked, "Grandma, what happened here?" Ayi, her voice laced with the wisdom of experience, began to tell him the story, weaving a cautionary tale of lost connection and the enduring power of a simple act of kindness. As the sun dipped below the horizon, casting long shadows on the dusty landscape, the boy listened intently, the faint digital hum a melancholic backdrop to a lesson learned. The story of the "Glitched Nine" would live on, a whisper in the wind, a reminder that true connection transcends the boundaries of the digital and the real.

THE RAIN BULL

Based on the African legend The Rain Bull.

The legend speaks to the encouraging story about the Rain Bull, who brings much-needed rain to the African plain.

In the sunbaked sprawl of Namibia, where the holographic sky shimmered with the relentless sun, and thirst was a constant notification, lived a young woman named Abeni. Renowned for her beauty and ability to hack her neural implant for witty comebacks, Abeni spent her days managing her family's cattle herd, their location blips flashing across her AR visor.

One scorching afternoon, a heavy silence descended upon the land. The once vibrant vegetation appeared faded on her AR display, and a low, mournful whine replaced the playful mooing of the calves. The life-giving rains, long overdue, seemed lost in the endless expanse of the simulated sky.

Parched and frustrated, Abeni climbed a massive termite mound, hoping to catch a network signal for a distant watering hole. Instead, she saw a glitch in the system - a distortion in the shimmering sky that resolved into the magnificent image of a bull. Its coat shimmered with an impossible sheen, reflecting the harsh sunlight, and its horns curved like two data streams. It was the legendary Rain Bull, a mythical anomaly in the system rumoured to hold the power to trigger weather simulations.

However, Abeni, unlike others who viewed the Rain Bull with awe, saw an opportunity. She knew what the parched land craved and wanted first access to any water source the Rain Bull might reveal. Ignoring the warnings of the village elders about respecting the system's integrity, Abeni approached the shimmering bull with a confident stride.

"Mighty Bull," she called out, her voice laced with a digital echo. "I heard you control the weather simulations. We need some rain here ASAP. My cattle are on the verge of becoming dehydrated data packets."

The Rain Bull turned its eyes to pools of shimmering code. Abeni expected a system crash but found only a flicker of amusement in the distorted image. "And how do you propose I initiate a rain simulation, young one?" it boomed, its voice a low hum that resonated through her implant.

"Well, wouldn't you need some incentive?" Abeni replied, a sly smile playing on her lips. "Maybe a juicy data offering? First access to the new water source simulation?"

The Rain Bull let out a sound resembling a corrupted file transfer, a glitch that shook the ground. "Incentive?" it boomed. "Do you think the weather simulations are a transaction, child? Rain comes when the land thirsts for life, not for your selfish desires."

Abeni scoffed. "The land needs life? Tell that to my parched throat and my malfunctioning cattle data."

The Rain Bull's image flickered sadly. With a final, distorted snort, it dissolved into a cascade of shimmering pixels. Disappointed but undeterred,

Abeni continued her search for water, a gnawing sense of unease twisting in her gut.

Days turned into weeks, and the drought intensified. The cattle's location blips grew fainter, their moans echoing Abeni's own deepening regret. Ashamed of her arrogance, she returned to the termite mound, a plea for forgiveness forming in her mind.

But to her surprise, a single, pixelated teardrop fell on her outstretched hand. Another followed it, and then another, until a gentle, digital rain began to fall across her AR visor. Looking towards the sky, Abeni saw a magnificent rainbow glitch through the simulated sky, a promise of renewed life in the system.

The rain simulation continued for days, replenishing the virtual landscape and bringing life back to the savanna. Abeni learned a harsh but valuable lesson: the rains were not a commodity to be hacked but a vital part of the simulated world, one to be cherished and respected. From then on, Abeni, the once proud girl, became a symbol of humility and a reminder that nature's bounty, even in its digital form, thrives on respect, not self-interest.

As the legend of the Rain Bull spread through the augmented reality network, it served as a call to cherish the delicate balance between humans and the simulated world. Years later, when Abeni was a wise old woman, the memory of her encounter with the Rain Bull remained vivid. She often recounted the tale to the younger generation; her voice laced with a quiet reverence for the digital world. The children, captivated by the story, would look up at the vast, simulated sky with newfound respect, understanding that rain was a gift, not a right and that respecting the system was essential for their continued existence. The legend of the Rain Bull, passed down through generations, became a powerful reminder of humanity's dependence on the delicate balance of their virtual world.

THE LION'S SHARE

Based on the African legend, The Lion's Share.

A fox joins the lion and donkey in hunting. When the donkey divides their catch into three equal portions, the angry lion kills the donkey and eats him. The fox then puts everything into one pile, leaving just a tiny bit for herself, and tells the lion to choose.

The air in the boardroom was thick with tension. Mr. Jabari, a powerful media mogul, sat at the head of the table, his gaze flitting between Aisha, the young tech entrepreneur, and Mr. Khan, the established media baron. A lucrative broadcasting deal lay on the table, the lion's share in the burgeoning digital market.

"Aisha, your app's innovative; I'll give you that," Jabari rumbled. "But let's face it: Khan Media has the infrastructure and the reach." He gestured towards Khan, who offered a smug smile.

"But Mr. Jabari," Aisha countered, her voice surprisingly steady, "innovation, not infrastructure, drives audiences today. Khan Media's empire is built on legacy content, while my app caters to the future."

Khan snorted. "The future? Your app is a gamble, a flimsy hare compared to my stable of proven gazelles."

Jabari's eyes narrowed. He disliked Khan's arrogance, but Khan's media empire was a proven cash cow. He considered the deal, weighing Khan's infrastructure against Aisha's cutting-edge technology.

Suddenly, Jabari's assistant burst in, a frantic expression on his face. "Sir, there's been a data breach! Khan Media's user base is plummeting!"

The smug smile vanished from Khan's face, replaced by a mask of horror. Jabari slammed his fist on the table. "What? How?"

Aisha felt a flicker of sympathy for the old lion, suddenly exposed and vulnerable. "Seems your gazelle, Mr. Khan, wasn't so stable after all," she said calmly.

Khan stammered, unable to meet Jabari's furious gaze. Jabari turned to Aisha, a new light sparking in his eyes.

"Ms. Hassan, I believe we have much to discuss," he said, his voice no longer a growl but a low, calculating purr.

Aisha leaned back in her chair, a steely glint in her eyes. She might have been the hare, but as the data breach showed, even the strongest lion could be brought down by a clever strategy. The question remained: would Jabari be a fair leader, or would he simply become another Khan, hungry for the lion's share? Only time would tell.

THE HOLE IN THE WALL

Based on the African Coffee Bay legend.
Local legend tells the story of a young woman who
falls in love with a sea deity. Their forbidden love
sparked the formation of the archway in the cliff.

The dusty backroads of the Eastern Cape stretched
endlessly before Themba. He gripped the steering
wheel of his beat-up Toyota, the air thick with
anticipation. On the passenger seat lay his phone,
buzzing with excited messages – "Hole in the Wall
Challenge: Accepted!"

Themba, a young entrepreneur with a flagging
tech start-up, had stumbled upon a viral sensation
– a daring app connecting investors with local
farmers seeking funding. But competition was
fierce. Tonight, he was on a mission: to convince
the Mhlakaza family, legendary cattle ranchers,
to participate in his app and revitalize their
struggling farm.

The farmhouse, a grand but weathered structure,
appeared on the horizon. Themba felt a knot

of nervousness tighten in his stomach. The Mhlakazas were known for their traditional ways and were resistant to modern technology. He was greeted by MaMhlakaza, a formidable woman with eyes that held the wisdom of generations. After a tense welcome, Themba presented his app, outlining a future where technology could bridge the gap between tradition and progress.

MaMhlakaza remained impassive. "We have our ways," she said curtly. "The land and the cattle, they sustain us. We don't need fancy apps."

Themba sensed a chance. He explained how the app could connect them with a wider market, securing better prices for their livestock. He spoke of building a legacy, not just for the farm, but for their family name.

MaMhlakaza seemed to consider his words. Then, her gaze hardened. "Our ancestors warn against outside forces disrupting the balance." She pointed towards a majestic rock formation in the distance, a giant hole carved through its centre – the Hole in the Wall.

Themba knew the legend. A false prophecy, fuelled by blind faith, had led to the MaMhlakazas culling their entire cattle herd, leaving them vulnerable to invasion. Now, he saw the fear in MaMhlakaza's eyes.

"Technology isn't an enemy," Themba said gently. "It's a tool. We can use it to honour our ancestors, not replace them."

Silence fell. The sun dipped below the horizon, painting the sky in fiery hues. Finally, MaMhlakaza spoke, her voice softer now. "We will consider it," she said. "But remember, young man, progress must respect the past."

Themba left with a hesitant hope. He hadn't secured a definite yes, but he hadn't received a flat-out no either. As he drove away, casting a final glance at the Hole in the Wall, a stark reminder hung in the air: blind faith in easy solutions could lead to greater hardship. The path forward, Themba realized, lay in finding a balance between tradition and technology, a lesson etched by history in the very landscape itself.

THE GHOST IN THE CASTLE

Based on the legend of the Ghost at the
Cape of Good Hope Castle in Cape Town.

The legend speaks of the ghost of a sad-faced woman wearing a long, grey cloak who walks through the Castle at night. Then there is the ghost who loves to join parties. It could be Lady Anne Barnard, who lived at the Castle for five years from 1797 while her husband was colonial secretary.

The skeletal remains of the Castle's forgotten past cast long shadows across the polished granite floor as Dr Ayo Makhaya pushed open the heavy oak door. An eerie silence hung in the air, broken only by the rhythmic squeak of her sneakers. Dr Makhaya, a renowned archaeologist, wasn't here for ghosts. She was after the truth – the truth buried beneath the very foundation of the Castle of Good Hope.

Legend spoke of a "Lady in Grey," a melancholic ghost forever trapped within the castle walls. Dr Makhaya wasn't a woman of superstition, but the recent discovery of a female skeleton unearthed during a renovation project piqued her curiosity. Could there be a connection?

Reaching the Governor's chambers, a room rumoured to be haunted by the vengeful spirit of Governor Pieter van Noodt, Dr Makhaya's heart hammered a little faster. The room was untouched by the renovations, a dusty time capsule. As she scanned the ornately carved desk, a low humming filled the room, emanating from an aged laptop forgotten in a corner.

Intrigued, Dr Makhaya powered it on. The screen flickered to life, revealing a series of encrypted messages and faded digital photos. One image, a woman in a grey dress with tear-stained cheeks, matched the descriptions of the Lady in Grey perfectly. Another photo, timestamped just days before the skeleton's estimated time of death, showed the woman standing beside a scowling, powerful-looking man. The caption simply read: "Noodt."

A wave of realization washed over Dr Makhaya. The Lady in Grey wasn't a ghost but a woman wronged by the tyrannical Governor. The encrypted messages hinted at a conspiracy to expose van Noodt's corruption. This wasn't a haunting but a digital plea for justice from beyond the grave.

News of Dr Makhaya's findings spread like wildfire. The encrypted messages were cracked, revealing a web of deceit and exploitation. A strange sensation filled the Castle as the truth about Governor van Noodt's reign came to light. The air felt lighter, the oppressive silence broken by the murmur of history finally being acknowledged.

A few months later, Dr Makhaya stood at the Governor's chamber window, gazing out at the bustling city lights. She felt the light, familiar touch against the back of her hand and stilled. She had been feeling this same sensation throughout her investigations about Noodt and the woman who had been slighted, the woman who many called the Lady in Grey. This time, she did not pull her hand away but waited. The feather-light touch slipped through her fingers and spanned across her palm to settle into what she could only simulate as a hand holding hers. She was holding her breath, and only when she felt the slight pressure of a squeeze enveloping her skin did she release the trapped air. Then it was gone. The temperature around her warmed, and she knew the Lady in Grey had thanked her and now could rest.

The Castle, once a symbol of fear, was now a testament to the power of uncovering the past. The legend of the Lady in Grey wasn't just dispelled; it was rewritten.

THE HYENA AND THE TWO ROADS

Based on the African story The Roads
that overcame the Hyena.

A very hungry hyena went out on the Tanzanian plains to hunt for food. He came to a branch in the bush road where the two paths veered off in different directions. He saw two goats caught in the thickets at the far end of the two different paths. With his mouth watering in anticipation, he decided that his left leg would follow the left path and his right leg the right path. He tried to follow them both simultaneously as the two paths continued to veer in different directions. Finally, he split in two. As the well-known African proverb says: Two roads overcame the hyena.

A nervous sweat slicked Amina's palms as she scrolled through social media. Two glowing job offers, both promising her dream career in tech, appeared on her screen. One was from her hometown startup, a scrappy underdog with a mission to revolutionize local agriculture. The other was from a sleek, international corporation offering a lucrative salary and a fancy title.

"Two paths," she muttered, echoing the proverb her grandmother used to tell her about the greedy hyena. Amina pictured the hyena, its body twisted by ambition, ultimately torn apart. She didn't want to be the hyena.

The international corporation's offer glittered like a mirage. The security, the prestige, the fast-track career – it was intoxicating. The startup's mission, while noble, seemed a little… quaint. Besides, who knew if they'd even succeed? Amina could almost hear the whispers of her ambitious college self-urging her towards the corporation.

Ignoring the tug at her heartstrings, Amina crafted a meticulously professional email, accepting the offer from the international corporation. Relief washed over her – a sense of having "made it." The future stretched before her, paved with luxury apartments and expensive vacations. She envisioned herself at the top, a powerful woman in the corporate jungle.

The reality, however, was far less glamorous. The

corporation was a well-oiled machine, but its cogs turned with a cold efficiency. Amina's days were filled with repetitive tasks, her creativity stifled by bureaucracy. The human impact of their work was shrouded in jargon and reports, leaving Amina feeling increasingly detached.

Months have turned into years. Amina climbed the corporate ladder, her pay checks growing fatter, and her apartment becoming more luxurious. Yet, with each promotion, a hollowness settled within her. The youthful spark she once possessed had dimmed, replaced by a cynical weariness. Colleagues who once seemed like potential friends became competitors in a cutthroat game.

One evening, scrolling through social media, Amina stumbled upon a news article about the local startup. Against all odds, they had achieved remarkable success. Their app had become a game-changer for local farmers, boosting their incomes and revolutionizing the agricultural landscape. Amina recognized some of the faces in the photos – the passionate young team that had filled her with such hope years ago.

A pang of regret, sharp and sudden, tore through her. What if? The question echoed in the sterile silence of her apartment. The corporation had fulfilled its promises – the money, the title, the prestige. But Amina realized it had come at a cost. It had stolen her purpose and passion, replacing them with a gnawing sense of emptiness.

Looking out at the city lights, Amina knew her journey wasn't over. The hyena story, she finally understood, wasn't just about choosing the right path at the beginning. Sometimes, the true test was in finding your way back, even if it meant starting over, even if it meant leaving behind the comfort of a gilded cage. The hollowness within her wasn't the end – it was a burning ember, a flicker of hope that perhaps, one day, she could find her way back to the path of purpose that wouldn't tear her apart but build her up, brick by brick.

THE MILKY WAY

Based on the African legend of how
the Milky Way came to be.

A strong-willed girl became so angry when her mother would not give her any of the delicious roasted roots that she grabbed the roasting roots from the fire and threw the roots and ashes into the sky, where the red and white roots now glow as red and white stars, and the ashes are the Milky Way. And there the road is to this day. Some people call it the Milky Way; some call it the Stars' Road, but no matter what you call it, it is the path made by a young girl many, many years ago who threw the bright sparks of her fire high up into the sky to make a road in the darkness.

Amara slammed her helmet shut, the metallic clang echoing in the cramped cockpit. Outside, the desolate landscape of Mars stretched endlessly, a rusty red tapestry pockmarked with abandoned mining outposts. A single tear traced a path down her cheek, blurring the holographic map projected on the inside of her helmet visor. This wasn't the future they envisioned. This wasn't the glittering utopia promised by the megacorporations that had lured them away from Earth.

Years ago, Earth had been a vibrant blue marble, cradling life in its warm embrace. Back then, Amara had been a defiant teenager, yearning for adventure beyond the confines of their small, resource-strapped village. Her grandmother, a wizened woman with eyes that held the wisdom of ages, had tried to warn her. "The stars," her grandmother used to say, "are not just points of light. They are fragments of a past forgotten, embers from a fire that once burned too bright."

Amara dismissed it as a relic of a bygone era. Earth's resources seemed infinite then. The megacorporations had been all too convincing with their slick advertisements and promises of a better life among the stars. Blinded by the illusion of boundless abundance, humanity had fallen prey to a collective delusion. They mined and plundered, leaving Earth a barren husk in their wake.

Now, here she was, marooned on a desolate rock with a handful of survivors – the grim remnants of a once-thriving colony. The anger that had fuelled her teenage rebellion now festered within her, a bitter taste on her tongue. Her rebellion, fuelled by naivety and a childish disregard for the wisdom of her elders, had inadvertently contributed to the very downfall she sought to escape.

One night, a different memory surfaced as Amara gazed at the Milky Way sprawling across the Martian sky—a memory of a blazing row with her grandmother. Amara had snatched a glowing ember from the village bonfire, the same fire that kept them warm and cooked their meagre meals. "I don't need your seeds, Nana," she'd yelled, hurling the ember into the night sky. "The future is up there!"

Now, looking at the Milky Way, Amara felt a shiver crawl down her spine. It wasn't a path anymore, as some called it – the "Stellar Road" – but a celestial scar—a constant reminder of their arrogance, a testament to the destructive power of unchecked greed.

But amidst the despair, a flicker of hope ignited. The ember she had thrown all those years ago wasn't simply a spark of rebellion. It symbolised a primordial will, a testament to the human spirit's ability to change. If these embers could blaze into the vast expanse of the night sky, couldn't humanity rekindle their connection with their planet, nurture it back to life?

The next day, Amara gathered the remaining survivors. She spoke of her grandmother's words, of the forgotten lessons locked within the legend of the burning embers. A new fire, kindled not by greed but by a desperate hope, flickered in their eyes.

They scavenged the wreckage of their failed colony, salvaging technology that could be repurposed. Hydroponic systems were cobbled together from old processing units. Seed banks, salvaged from an abandoned corporate research facility, offered a glimmer of promise.

It was slow, arduous work. Every sprout was a victory, every drop of recycled water a small step towards a future they barely dared dream of. Yet, as the first green shoots unfurled inside the makeshift biodome, a feeling of community stronger than any they'd known before blossomed amongst them.

News of their endeavour trickled through the vast network of interplanetary colonies, sparking a quiet revolution. As they came to be known, the story of the "Burned Ember Colony" resonated with others who were tired of the empty promises and unsustainable practices of the megacorporations.

Amara, no longer the rebellious teenager, emerged as a symbol of hope. She wasn't a leader in the traditional sense but a catalyst, a reminder of the lessons etched in the celestial canvas of the Milky Way. They had taken, they had exploited, and they had reaped the consequences. It was time to learn from the past to cultivate a future where humanity and nature co-existed in a delicate balance.

Years later, as a fragile ecosystem began to take root on Mars, Amara looked out at the Milky Way. No longer a symbol of despair, it was a beacon of inspiration – a reminder of their mistakes, the resilience of life, and the enduring power of hope that burned brighter than any forgotten ember. The future wasn't fixed; it was a story they were rewriting with every seed sown, every drop of water recycled, and every step they took towards a new beginning. The embers may have been a symbol of their destruction, but they had also become the spark of their redemption. The Burned Ember Colony's success became a beacon across the star systems. Corporations, pressured by a growing public consciousness and dwindling resources, began investing in sustainable practices. Green initiatives sprouted across abandoned colonies, and the once-exploited planets started showing signs of regeneration.

Amara, however, remained vigilant. The corporations, she knew, were creatures of habit. They needed a constant push towards responsible resource management. With this in mind, she decided to use the very network they had created to their advantage.

She, along with a team of talented programmers and engineers, created the "Ember Protocol." This code, hidden within the data streams of the interplanetary network, subtly influenced corporate algorithms towards sustainable practices. It encouraged the use of renewable energy, promoted resource efficiency, and even penalized environmentally destructive mining strategies.

Unaware of the subtle manipulation, the corporations found themselves inexplicably drawn towards renewable energy solutions and ethical resource management. It felt like a sudden shift in market forces, a mysterious economic trend they couldn't quite explain.

Meanwhile, the Burned Ember Colony flourished. Lush greenery replaced the rusty red landscape.

New generations were born and raised on stories of the past and their responsibility to the future. They became pioneers of terraforming technology, sharing their knowledge with other struggling colonies.

Decades later, Amara, now a revered elder, stood before a gathering of young colonists. The Milky Way shimmered above them, a tapestry of stars and hope. "Remember," she said, her voice soft but firm, "the embers remind us of two things. Greed can consume and destroy, but so can a rebellious spirit. Learn from the past, but don't let anger guide your future. Let the embers be a testament to the human capacity for destruction and creation."

A young boy, no older than ten, stepped forward. "Nana Amara," he asked, eyes filled with curiosity, "what if the corporations figure out the Ember Protocol?"

A gentle smile graced Amara's lip. "By then, my dear," she said, "they will have learned a different lesson. They will have learned that true progress isn't about endless consumption, but about fostering a sustainable harmony with the worlds we inhabit."

As they gazed at the Milky Way, no longer a celestial scar but a canvas of possibilities, they knew the embers, once a symbol of folly, had ignited a revolution. A revolution that had transformed the stars from a reminder of a lost home into a promise of a thriving future. In that moment, under the watchful gaze of the galaxy, a new chapter in humanity's cosmic journey began.

THE SUN

Based on the African story about The Sun.

The Sun was once a man who made it day when he raised his arms, for a powerful light shone from his armpits. But as he grew old and slept too long, the people grew cold. Children crept up on him and threw him into the sky, where he became round and has stayed warm and bright ever since. Some believed that after sunset, the sun travelled back to the east over the top of the sky and that the stars are small holes which let the light through. Others said that the sun is eaten each night by a crocodile and emerges from it each morning. According to a Naron bushman, the Sun turned into a rhinoceros at sunset, killed and eaten by the people in the west. They then throw the shoulder blade towards the east, where it turns into an animal again and starts to rise.

Dr Mbeki stared out the window of his sterile lab, the ever-present glow of artificial suns casting an eerie light within. Outside, the real sun, a fading ember choked by pollution, was a distant memory.

Mbeki, the lead scientist on Project Helios, had promised a sustainable future powered by controlled fusion, but years of chasing limitless energy backfired. They'd become dependent on the artificial suns, neglecting the real ones. Now, the planet was shrouded in a constant, sickly twilight, the sky a polluted canvas devoid of stars.

He recalled his grandmother's folktales of the Sun, a powerful human who provided warmth and light. Mbeki had dismissed them as primitive myths. Now, he understood them as cautionary tales. In its insatiable pursuit of power, humanity had played the role of the mischievous children, unknowingly dimming the Sun.

A new urgency filled Mbeki. Project Helios needed a new direction. The focus wouldn't just be on energy creation but on environmental restoration. They'd clean the atmosphere, allowing the real Sun to reclaim its rightful place.

It would be a long, arduous journey, but one Mbeki was determined to take. He wouldn't let humanity remain trapped in the artificial twilight of their own making. The folktale, once a whimsical story, became a blueprint for redemption. The Sun, though weakened, still had the power to heal. It was time to appease the Sun, not exploit it, to learn to live in harmony with its light, not replace it. The future wouldn't be powered by limitless, artificial suns but by a restored Sun and a renewed respect for its power. The cost of defying the natural order was a lesson Mbeki wouldn't allow humanity to forget.

DEATH

Based on the African story of
how death came to be.

The Moon, it is said, sent once an Insect to Men, saying, "Go thou to Men, and tell them, 'As I die, and dying live, so ye shall also die, and dying live.'" The Insect started with the message but, whilst on his way, was overtaken by the Hare, who asked: "On what errand art thou bound? "The Insect answered: "I am sent by the Moon to Men, to tell them that as she dies, and dying lives, they also shall die, and dying live." The Hare said, "As thou art an awkward runner, let me go" (to take the message). With these words, he ran off, and when he reached Men, he said, "I am sent by the Moon to tell you, 'As I die, and dying to perish, in the same manner, ye shall also die and come wholly to an end.'" Then the Hare returned to the Moon and told her what he had said to Men. The Moon reproached him angrily, saying, "Darest thou tell the people a thing which I have not said? She took up a piece of wood with these words and struck him on the nose. Since that day, Hare's nose is slit.

Ayo, a young programmer with eyes that mirrored the twinkling night sky, raced his sleek motorbike down the dusty road. The wind whipped through his braids, carrying the distant rhythm of the village drumming. Tonight was the annual Egungun Festival, a vibrant celebration to honour the ancestors. Ayo's heart thumped with anticipation; besides the festivities, he was on his way to meet his grandmother, Nneka, a woman who whispered to possess the wisdom of the ancient baobab trees.

Nneka lived on the outskirts of the village in a quaint mud hut adorned with colourful calabashes. Ayo found her by the flickering firelight, her weathered face etched with stories of a bygone era. As the crackling flames cast dancing shadows, Ayo poured her a cup of steaming hibiscus tea.

"Tell me, Nneka," Ayo began, his voice laced with curiosity, "is it true what they say about Oduduwa, the first of our kind? That he lived forever?"

Nneka chuckled a low rumble that belied her diminutive frame. "Forever, my child? Even the stars eventually fade," she said, her eyes twinkling with mischief. "But there's a story, passed down through generations, about how death came to be."

Ayo leaned closer, captivated. Nneka's voice softened as she began:

"Long ago, in a time before smartphones and the internet, our ancestors lived in harmony with nature. They believed the Moon, a wise and benevolent spirit, watched over them. One day, the Moon, fearing the world would become overpopulated, decided to send a message to humanity."

She paused, sipping her tea. "The chosen messenger was a humble cricket, his chirping a familiar song in the night. The Moon entrusted him with a message: 'As I wax and wane, so too shall all life experience a cycle of change. Even I, the Moon, must eventually rest.'"

Ayo nodded, understanding the cyclical nature she described.

"But the cricket, a creature known for his timidness," Nneka continued, a glint in her eyes, "was overtaken on his journey by the cunning tortoise, Ayo's namesake. The tortoise craved the honour of delivering such an important message."

"Ayo, the tortoise?" Ayo exclaimed, a laugh bubbling up from his chest. Nneka smiled.

"Yes," she said, "This Ayo, ever the braggart, decided to embellish the message. He reached the village and declared, 'The Moon warns you! As she disappears each night, so too will you vanish forever!'"

A gasp escaped Ayo's lips. "Oh no!"

"Indeed," Nneka said. "Furious at the twisted message, the Moon struck Ayo with a celestial beam, leaving a permanent crack on his shell. Death, this unwelcome change, was not the Moon's initial plan, but a consequence of the tortoise's ego."

Ayo sat in thoughtful silence. The crackling fire seemed to whisper the tortoise's folly. He realized the story wasn't just about the origin of death but about the responsibility of communication.

"So, death is inevitable?" he finally asked.

Nneka's eyes held a quiet wisdom. "All things change, Ayo. Life, like the moon, has its phases. But even in death, our ancestors become part of the earth, nourishing the soil for new life to spring forth. We must cherish our time and purpose and leave a legacy honouring those who came before us."

Ayo rose, his heart brimming with a newfound understanding. He thanked Nneka and rode back to the village, the rhythmic drumming now a symphony of remembrance. The Egungun Festival, he realized, wasn't just a celebration but a way to bridge the gap between the living and the dead, a testament to the interconnectedness of all things. As the vibrant masks danced under the watchful gaze of the Moon, Ayo knew he would carry Nneka's story with him, a reminder of the delicate balance of life and the importance of living every moment to its fullest.

THE SEVEN MAGIC BIRDS

Based on the African story, The Seven Magic Birds.

The legend tells the story of the father who
longs for his grown sons only to find joy
within the son who is left behind.

The concrete jungle of Soweto seemed to shimmer in the relentless midday sun. Sixteen-year-old Siphiwe sat on his rickety stoop, fiddling with his broken phone. He dreamt of escaping the dusty streets, of a life filled with more than fixing scrap metal and scavenging for parts. He longed for the digital world his phone could barely access.

Suddenly, a flurry of movement caught his eye. Seven swallows, unlike any he'd ever seen, swooped down. Their feathers shimmered with an otherworldly sheen – blue like the summer sky, infused with streaks of gold like sunlight on water. Curiosity replaced his initial shock, and Siphiwe followed them.

The birds led him on a wild chase through the labyrinthine alleyways, past bustling street vendors and graffiti-laden walls. Finally, they landed on a weathered billboard overlooking a dusty soccer field. The faded and cracked advertisement depicted a bustling tech conference, a world far removed from his own.

Intrigued, Siphiwe reached out. As his hand brushed a feather, the picture on the billboard flickered, and a holographic image materialized. It was an old woman, her eyes sparkling with wisdom. "You have been chosen, Siphiwe," she said, her voice a melodic hum. "These birds will guide you, each holding a piece of the knowledge you seek."

With that, the image dissolved, and the birds chirped excitedly. One after another, they flew off. Siphiwe hesitantly followed, each bird leading him to a different part of Soweto he'd never explored before. One led him to a hidden community centre with a free coding class, another to a rooftop where a group of teenagers hacked Wi-Fi signals, their laptops glowing in the twilight. Each encounter was a puzzle piece, unlocking a new skill or revealing a hidden resource.

Days turned into weeks, and Siphiwe's skills blossomed. He learned to code, build his website, troubleshoot his broken phone, and even turn it into a rudimentary scanner. He connected with the hidden tech communities of Soweto, a vibrant network of young minds hacking their way into the digital world.

One day, the seven swallows returned, leading him back to the billboard. This time, the holographic image depicted a young man, eyes gleaming with ambition, standing on a stage at the very tech conference on the billboard. He held a sleek device, glowing with the same blue and gold as the swallows' feathers.

"This is your future, Siphiwe," the old woman's voice resonated. "Your journey has just begun. Use your skills and knowledge to build a bridge between your world and the one you dreamt of."

Siphiwe smiled, a newfound determination burning in his eyes. He no longer yearned to escape Soweto. He saw it – the dusty streets, the community centres, the hidden corners – as the foundation for his future. With his newfound knowledge, he could bridge the digital divide, bringing tech opportunities to his community and showing them that the world he dreamt of wasn't so far away after all.

The legend of the seven magic birds became a whisper in Soweto's digital underground, a reminder that the most valuable resources are often hidden in plain sight, waiting to be discovered by those with the courage to follow the unexpected. And guess what Siphiwe named his first tech company? The Seven Magic Swallows.

However, Siphiwe's journey was far from over. The digital world was vast and ever evolving, and there were always new bridges to be built. He knew that the swallows might return someday, leading him on new adventures, teaching him new skills, and reminding him that the most important lesson wasn't just about technology but about the power of community and the potential that lies within his backyard.

MAPANDANGARE, THE GREAT BABOON

Based on the African legend
Mapandangare, the Great Baboon.

The story shows how a baboon helps a herder
girl to protect her cattle, sheep and goats.

Asuma rubbed sweat from her brow, her gaze fixed on the flickering screen of her tablet. Her cattle app, a lifeline for her small ranch in rural South Africa, displayed a grim picture: plummeting livestock prices combined with a skyrocketing feed cost. Panic gnawed at her. How could she compete with the giant agricultural corporations without losing everything?

Suddenly, a guttural screech echoed across the dusty plains. Asuma shielded her eyes as a massive shadow fell over her. It was a creature straight out of legend – a colossal baboon, its fur the colour of burnt umber, its eyes glinting with intelligence. A gold chain, a jarring modern touch, dangled from its neck.

Asuma froze, her heart pounding against her ribs. Legends called him Mapandangare, the Great Baboon, a mythical protector of the land. But could he be real? She touched the packet of dagga cookies her friend had left for her just minutes earlier. Could she be imagining this …

The large baboon, ignoring her apprehension, opened his mouth, and to Asuma's astonishment, a perfectly calibrated voice boomed from within. "Asuma of the failing herd? Your distress echoes across the land."

Asuma, speechless, could only nod. The baboon chuckled a low rumble that surprised her. "You fight a losing battle, child. The modern market devours the small. But fret not, for Mapandangare offers an alternative."

He nudged her tablet with a massive finger, a surprisingly agile feat. A new app icon materialized – a stylized baboon head. Hesitantly, Asuma tapped it. An explosion of information flooded the screen: local farmer co-ops, organic farming techniques, direct-to-consumer marketing strategies.

"This app," Mapandangare rumbled, "is your key to a new path. Unite with your fellow farmers. Embrace traditional knowledge. Forge a connection with your customers."

Asuma's scepticism gave way to a spark of hope. This was a chance, unconventional but real. "But why me?" she asked.

Mapandangare winked, or at least she thought he did. "You have a fire in your belly, little one. And sometimes, the greatest strength lies in the unexpected." He gestured with his head towards the departing sun. "The choice is yours."

As dusk painted the sky in hues of orange and purple, Mapandangare vanished as mysteriously as he arrived. Asuma, filled with newfound resolve, started working. She contacted farmers from neighbouring villages, shared the app's information, and organized online communities. The Baboon Head app spread like wildfire, igniting a movement for sustainable agriculture and direct-to-consumer sales.

Months later, Asuma stood in a bustling marketplace, her stall overflowing with fresh produce. Farmers, once rivals, now collaborated.

Consumers, tired of mass-produced food, flocked to them, drawn by the promise of quality and ethical sourcing. Asuma, looking up at the bright sun, smiled. Maybe legends weren't just stories after all. Sometimes, all you needed was a giant, internet-savvy baboon to point you in the right direction.

THE SNAKE

Based on the African legend, The Snake that bit the Girl.

The story follows the journey of villagers striving to get revenge against the snake who bit a girl and how, in the end, the snake receives his dues.

Ayo slumped against the chipped enamel pot, beads of sweat clinging to her forehead. Lagos simmered under the unrelenting afternoon sun, and with it, so did her anger. Why was she, a university student burdened with part-time jobs, responsible for feeding her entire family after their father – that irresponsible snake – had gotten himself arrested again? Baba had sauntered in just days ago, his usual swagger replaced by a sheepish grin and a flimsy story about a "misunderstanding" with the police. As always, He'd brought trouble, leaving Ayo to scramble for the family's survival.

Suddenly, a thud on the corrugated iron roof startled her. She whirled around, her heart hammering against her ribs. A man, lean and muscular, stood before her, a mischievous glint in his eyes. He moved with an unnatural grace like a predator sizing up its prey.

"You must be Ayo," he said, his voice a smooth murmur. "Your father sends his apologies and… a gift."

He gestured towards a steaming bowl in his hand. Ayo's stomach growled, the scent of rich egusi soup filling the air. But with Baba's history of shady dealings, mistrust gnawed at her.

"What's in it?" she demanded, refusing to reach for the bowl.

The man's smile faltered. "Just a token of appreciation," he mumbled. "The best egusi your mother could find."

Ayo studied him, doubt etching lines on her brow. Then, the rumble in her stomach decided for her. She snatched the bowl and slammed the rickety door shut, leaving the man muttering outside. Whether this was from her very dead mother, or it was a sick sales pitch, her belly ached with too many days of no food to care for.

The soup was heavenly. Each mouthful was a warm embrace, a memory of her mother's gentle touch. But as the sun dipped below the horizon, the egusi started to churn in her stomach. A wave of nausea hit her, followed by a burning sensation that spread from her insides outwards. Ayo doubled over, gasping for breath.

Her screams tore through the evening air, jolting the neighbours awake. They burst through the door to find Ayo writhing on the floor, frothing at the mouth. The bowl of egusi lay overturned beside her, a sinister stain marring the floorboards.

Frantic calls to the hospital fell on deaf ears. The city's generators sputtered, plunging the neighbourhood into darkness. With each agonizing breath, Ayo realized this soup wasn't a gift but a punishment. But not from the police. Maybe this time, Baba had finally crossed the wrong path, and the consequences were hotter than any soup.

As Ayo's vision blurred, the screams of her neighbours turned into a distant echo. The snake had returned, not in the form of a mythical being, but a slick man with a poisoned gift. And unlike the ancient stories, no potent soup would vanquish him. His own actions would consume him, leaving his daughter and family to pay the ultimate price for his poisonous legacy.

The following days were a blur of frantic activity. Ayo's friends rallied around her, taking turns at her bedside and keeping a watchful eye on her younger siblings. News of the poisoning spread through the close-knit community, and a wave of anger towards Baba rose. The whispers turned into action – men from the neighbourhood volunteered to patrol the streets at night, and women pooled their resources to ensure Ayo's family wouldn't go hungry.

Ayo recovered slowly, the ordeal leaving her physically and emotionally drained. But amidst the hardship, she saw a flicker of hope. The community's unwavering support reminded her that she wasn't alone. This wasn't just her burden to bear. It was a time for them to come together, to rise above the chaos Baba had created.

With newfound determination, Ayo started attending night classes again. She devoured her studies, fuelled by a desire to build a future not just for herself but for her siblings. The experience had hardened her resolve, transforming her anger into a burning ambition. She would break free from the cycle of poverty and irresponsibility that had plagued her family for generations. The memory of the poisoned soup served as a constant reminder – a bitter lesson that fuelled her fight for a better life.

AFTER LIFE

Based on Zulu legends about the After Life.

Bushmen appear to have had a belief in an afterlife. A dead man's weapons were buried with him, and his face was turned to the rising sun, as they believed that were he to face the west, it would take the sun longer to rise the next day. For burial, the bodies were sometimes anointed with a red powder and melted fat. They were then placed in shallow graves, in a curled-up position – the favourite sleeping posture of man in life. Some African tribes would break the bones of their dead upon internment (perhaps to deter their ghosts from walking and wandering around), but the Bushmen never did this. They allowed the corpse to remain intact and merely raised a small cairn of stones over it to prevent wild beasts from scratching.

Xenia, a young anthropologist, had spent years studying the Kung people, a modern-day descendant of the Bushmen, in the Kalahari Desert. Their vibrant culture, particularly their beliefs about the afterlife, fascinated her. Unlike other tribes, the Kung didn't fear death. They believed the deceased simply returned to the earth, their spirits joining the whispering wind and dancing dust devils.

One scorching afternoon, news came that Xau, the tribe's elder and Xenia's dearest friend, had passed. The ceremony was unlike any funeral Xenia had witnessed. Instead of mourning, the Kung celebrated Xau's life with joyous songs and rhythmic clapping. They buried him facing the rising sun, a red ochre paste painted on his wrinkled face.

Later that night, as Xenia sat by the crackling fire, a cool breeze swirled around her, carrying the faint scent of Xau's pipe tobacco. A shiver ran down her spine. Looking up, she saw a familiar figure standing amidst the star-dusted night sky. It was Xau, his eyes twinkling with amusement.

Xenia gasped, her heart hammering against her ribs. "B-but… how?" she stammered.

Xau chuckled, a dry, raspy sound. "The wind carries my spirit, little one. I came to say goodbye."

Relief washed over Xenia, replaced by a bittersweet pang. They talked for hours, Xau sharing stories from his youth, his voice carried on the desert breeze. As the first rays of dawn painted the sky, Xau faded, his form dissolving into the rising sun.

Days turned into weeks; the memory of Xau's visit was a cherished secret. Then, one evening, while reviewing her notes, Xenia noticed something peculiar. A sketch she'd made of a constellation, a formation the Kung called "The Dancing Spirit," bore an uncanny resemblance to how Xau had stood that night. Suddenly, it dawned on her. The Kung didn't believe their dead returned as ghosts, but as part of the very fabric of the universe, their spirits were woven into the constellations, forever watching over them.

Xenia understood then. Death wasn't an ending but a transformation, a beautiful twist in the circle of life. In their wisdom, the Kung had found a way to celebrate life and the enduring connection that transcended even death. This realization sparked a fire within Xenia. She decided to share Kung's philosophy with the world, hoping to offer a new perspective on death that embraced acceptance and the beauty of the eternal cycle.

Back in her academic circles, Xenia's findings were met with scepticism. "Primitive beliefs," some scoffed. But Xenia persisted, weaving tales of Xau's farewell and the constellation that mirrored his form. Slowly, a shift in perception began. People started to see Kung's beliefs not as primitive but as a profound acceptance of the natural order.

Xenia's lectures became sought after. She spoke of the Kungs' reverence for the night sky and how they saw deceased loved ones not as lost but as guiding stars. Her work sparked conversations about grief, loss, and the impermanence of life. Many found solace in Kung's philosophy, a perspective that offered comfort and a sense of continuity beyond the physical world.

Xenia continued her research, delving deeper into the Kung's spiritual practices. She documented their star songs, their rituals for honouring the dead, and their deep connection to the natural world. Her work became a bridge between cultures, offering a window into a way of life that celebrated the cycle of existence, from the first breath to the final sigh and the starlit eternity that followed.

THE HITCHHIKER

Based on the African ghost story
The Spectral Hitchhiker.

In the Great Karoo, not far from Uniondale on the national road, there is a turn-off that leads to Barandas. Here, no one will pick up a hitchhiker – especially a girl – around Easter, for it is at that time that a young girl stands hitchhiking at the roadside, dressed in dark slacks and shirt. She has accepted a lift from many an unsuspecting motorist – only to leave them, suddenly and inexplicably, 17 km further on, at the next turn-off to Barandas.

The dusty windshield of Liam's beat-up bakkie reflected the relentless Karoo sun. He squinted at the endless stretch of parched earth, the radio a symphony of static. His phone had died hours ago, leaving him utterly alone with the desolate beauty of the South African heartland.

Suddenly, a figure emerged from the shimmering heat haze: a young woman with dark hair plastered to her forehead by sweat. She held a dented backpack and wore clothes better suited for the city streets than the unforgiving Karoo.

Liam pulled over, a flicker of concern tugging at his heart. "Need a lift?" he called out.

Relief flooded the woman's face. "Thank heavens! My car broke down miles back, and I've been stranded all afternoon."

Liam helped her load her backpack into the back and studied her in the rearview mirror, a little niggle pulsating in his brain that he had not seen any abandoned car on his drive so far."Where are you headed, then?"

"Uniondale," she replied, her voice surprisingly calm.

Liam chuckled. "Uniondale? In the middle of nowhere? You sure you got the right town?"

"Positive," she smiled, a touch too wide for his liking. "I have… family there."

Liam shrugged. Hitchhikers were rare in these parts, especially the female kind, but he wasn't one to judge. He flicked on some music, trying to break the ice-cold silence that settled between them.

The woman remained strangely quiet as the sun dipped below the horizon, painting the sky in fiery hues. Her eyes were fixed on a distant point, with a look of unsettling detachment. Liam felt a prickle of unease crawl up his spine, wishing he had asked her to sit up front with him.

He noticed that she kept glancing down at a paper in her hands. It looked like a faded map, and he managed to see the words Uniondale heavily marked through the back window. He also saw a flash of a strange symbol, a swirling vortex of black and white, seemingly drawn over the town itself.

"What's that?" he asked, gesturing at the map.

The woman's smile returned, wider this time, chillingly manic. "Just a little something to remember the place by."

Suddenly, a gust of icy wind swept through the car despite the closed windows, sending shivers down Liam's spine. The radio sputtered and died, plunging them into an even deeper silence.

He glanced back at the woman. Her features had morphed, her once youthful face now etched with age and malevolence. Her eyes glowed an eerie white devoid of warmth.

"You see," she rasped, her voice a guttural whisper, "I don't need a lift. Uniondale needs me. And soon, you will, too."

Liam slammed on the brakes, panic clawing at his throat. But the car wouldn't stop. It lurched forward, accelerating on its own. The howling wind swallowed his screams as the vehicle veered off the road, heading straight for the heart of the Karoo, towards the ominous symbol marked on the map. The ghostly hitchhiker's laughter echoing in the night vanished without a trace.

The next morning, Liam's abandoned bakkie was found near a remote part of the Karoo. There was no sign of life or any sign of a struggle. The map lay crumpled on the passenger seat, the black and white vortex pulsating faintly as if beckoning another unsuspecting soul.

Days turned into weeks, then months, with no sign of Liam. Whispers of the strange disappearance spread through the close-knit Karoo communities. Search parties scoured the vast landscape but found nothing. Liam's family, wracked with grief and clinging to hope, refused to believe he was gone.

One starlit night, a lone figure emerged from the swirling dust on the outskirts of Uniondale. It was a haggard man, his clothes tattered, his face weathered by the harsh elements. His eyes, however, held a glint of determination. It was Liam. He had somehow escaped the clutches of the supernatural hitchhiker, but the experience had left him forever changed.

The swirling vortex on the map had become a burning memory, a constant reminder of the darkness that lurked beneath the Karoo's beauty. Yet, it had also ignited a spark within him - a thirst for knowledge about the hidden forces at play.

Liam spent years researching local folklore and legends, piecing together fragments of a forgotten lore. He learned about a hidden realm accessible through portals scattered across the Karoo, some benign, others harbouring entities like the one he encountered. He discovered that the black-and-white vortex was a marker, a warning sign for those who dared to trespass.

Liam, driven by a mix of survivor's guilt and a newfound obsession, built a website. He meticulously documented his experience, uploading the faded map with the pulsing vortex prominently displayed. He titled the site "The Karoo Chronicles: Don't Pick Up Hitchhikers."

At first, the site languished in the digital wasteland. Then, a flurry of activity. Comments flooded the page, ranging from sceptical mockery to chillingly similar encounters. Liam connected with others who had glimpsed the spectral hitchhiker or encountered the strange portals. A small online community of survivors formed, sharing their experiences and piecing together the Karoo's hidden secrets.

One day, a new message arrived. It wasn't text but a video. Shaky and filled with static, a grainy clip showed a lone figure standing in front of the black-and-white vortex. It was Liam, his face gaunt, eyes filled with a manic intensity.

"The warnings were wrong," he rasped, his voice distorted by the static. "Uniondale needs saving. We are the key. Join us."

The video abruptly cut off. Panic clawed at Liam's online community. Days turned into weeks, then months—no further messages from Liam. The website remained a chilling testament to the Karoo's secrets and a beacon, perhaps, for others like Liam, drawn to the darkness that pulsed faintly beneath the digital map.

THE VISITOR

Based loosely on the African Story of the Visitor.

Just below the Swartberg Pass summit ridge lurks the ruins of a building, sparsely protected from the bitter winds by a straggling grove of pine trees. This is the ruin of the old tollhouse originally built to house convict labourers employed on the construction of the road between 1881 and 1888 by Thomas Bain, son of the famous Andrew Geddes Bain, who was responsible for Bain's Kloof Pass in the Western Cape.

The icy spray of sleet stung Theo's face as he huddled under the crumbling archway of the old tollhouse. The wind howled like a banshee, carrying with it the mournful cry of a distant jackal. He'd been foolish, he knew, to attempt the Swartberg Pass in the throes of a winter storm. Now, stranded and alone, he wished he'd heeded the locals' warnings about the "Spookhuis" – the haunted tollhouse. Yet, here he was, taking shelter from the storm in that very house.

Just as despair threatened to paralyze him, a soft rapping echoed from inside the ruined building.

Relief washed over Theo. Maybe he wasn't alone after all. Pushing aside a heavy wooden door, he found himself in a dimly lit room, debris littering the damp floor. Huddled in the corner, his back turned, sat a figure cloaked in a dark, tattered coat.

While he should have been alarmed and afraid, Theo was not prone to believing in ghost stories and prided himself on being quite practical. In broken Afrikaans, Theo explained his predicament, offering a grateful smile. The figure remained silent, unmoving. Theo ventured closer, offering a steaming mug of coffee he'd managed to brew with a camp stove.

The figure turned. Its face, obscured by the hood, remained shrouded in shadow. But its eyes, two glowing embers in the gloom, held Theo captive. Panic seized him. There was an unnatural stillness to the figure, a cold emptiness that sent shivers down his spine.

He stammered a question, a plea for assistance, but the only response was a low, guttural moan. The figure rose, its form impossibly tall and skeletal. It moved towards him, an icy breath chilling Theo to the bone.

Instinct finally took over. Theo scrambled back, tripping and falling over debris. He fumbled for his phone, but its screen remained stubbornly black. With a final, desperate glance back, he bolted out into the storm, the relentless wind carrying the chilling echo of the figure's mournful moan.

The next morning, the sun peeked through the clouds, casting an ethereal glow on the desolate landscape. Theo, exhausted but alive, reached the bottom of the Swartberg Pass. He glanced back at the tollhouse, perched on the distant mountain ridge like a skeletal sentinel. The wind seemed to whisper a chilling message – "He is still waiting."

Back in the safety of civilization, Theo couldn't shake the feeling of being watched. The image of the figure's glowing eyes haunted his dreams. Was it a figment of his storm-addled mind? A product of fear and hypothermia? Or was it something more? Something waiting for the next unsuspecting visitor to seek shelter within the haunted walls of the Spookhuis?

Unable to quell his unease, Theo decided to do some research. He scoured online forums and historical archives, piecing together the fragmented history of the tollhouse. He learned that it had been abandoned decades ago after a series of unexplained disappearances. A local legend spoke of a vengeful toll collector who met a grisly end at the hands of outlaws, forever bound to the site.

Theo, however, wasn't convinced by the supernatural explanation. He suspected something more sinister at play. He revisited the online forums, this time focusing on those dedicated to unexplained phenomena and paranormal investigations. There, he found a user named "KarooSeeker", who claimed to have had a similar encounter at the Spookhuis.

Theo messaged KarooSeeker, sharing his own experience and suspicions. To his surprise, he received a prompt response. KarooSeeker, whose real name was Sarah, revealed that she was a data analyst fascinated with the unexplained. She had been investigating the disappearances at the Spookhuis for years, convinced there was a more rational explanation.

Theo and Sarah began exchanging messages regularly, comparing notes and piecing together the puzzle. Sarah had discovered a pattern in the disappearances – all the missing people had been hikers or bikers who had attempted the Swartberg Pass during winter storms, forcing them to seek shelter at the tollhouse.

"There has to be another explanation," Sarah messaged Theo. "Maybe an environmental factor – carbon monoxide poisoning from a faulty chimney or something?"

Theo wasn't so sure. He recounted the unnatural stillness of the figure, the cold that seemed to radiate from it. He also mentioned the glowing eyes, a detail Sarah found particularly intriguing.

"Perhaps there's some kind of technology involved," she mused. "Maybe a holographic projection or some sort of energy field that creates these illusions."

The idea sparked a fire in Theo. He began researching experimental military technology and stumbled upon a project codenamed "Project Umbra."

The details were scarce, but it seemed to focus on cloaking technology and advanced prosthetics. A shiver ran down Theo's spine. Could Project Umbra be the answer? Was the figure at the Spookhuis a prototype soldier, lost and malfunctioning in the harsh mountain environment?

He reached out to Sarah, his message laced with urgency. "Look into Project Umbra," he typed frantically. "I think we're onto something big."

Days turned into weeks, their investigation hitting dead ends. Frustration gnawed at Theo, but Sarah remained undeterred. Finally, a breakthrough. She unearthed a heavily redacted document referencing a secret military base located deep within the Swartberg Mountains. The base, codenamed "Shadowfall," coincided perfectly with the location of the Spookhuis.

A combination of excitement and terror coursed through Theo. They were on the right track, but the implications were terrifying. Were these rogue soldiers, or was something more sinister at play? Theo knew they couldn't investigate alone. He convinced Sarah to reach out to a journalist known for tackling government conspiracies.

Going public was a gamble, but Theo felt it was their only option. The journalist, sceptical at first, was intrigued by their findings. He agreed to meet them at a pre-arranged location near the

Swartberg Pass. Armed with Theo's photos from the Spookhuis and Sarah's compiled data, they laid out their case.

The journalist listened intently, a flicker of determination in his eyes. He promised to investigate, to get the truth out there. A weight lifted from Theo's shoulders. He had done what he could. Now, he could only wait and pray that their story would see the light of day and that the secrets buried within the desolate walls of the Spookhuis would finally be exposed.

THE WOMAN AND THE SNAKE

Based on the African story, The
White Man and the Snake.

A white man, it is said, met a Snake upon whom a large
stone had fallen and covered her so that she could
not rise. The White Man lifted the stone off Snake,
but when he had done so, she wanted to bite him.

Dr Amelia Turner, a renowned primatologist,
trekked through the dense rainforest, her boots
sinking into the damp earth. She was on the
trail of a rare primate, the elusive golden-crowned
mangabey. The humid air hung thick, a symphony
of buzzing insects and screeching birds filling the
air.

Suddenly, a rustle in the undergrowth caught her
attention. Squinting through the leafy canopy,
Amelia spotted a flash of emerald scales. It was
a serpent, its body impossibly long and thick, its
head shimmering a vibrant green. But something

was wrong. The massive snake was trapped, its body pinned beneath a fallen log.

Amelia's heart clenched. Despite her initial fear, a wave of compassion washed over her. She knew this was a once-in-a-lifetime encounter, a chance to study a creature of myth and legend. But the snake's predicament couldn't be ignored.

Carefully, she inched closer, her movements deliberate. The snake watched her approach, its forked tongue flicking in and out, a warning sign Amelia chose to ignore. With practised motions, she assessed the situation. With a deep breath, she reached out and, with surprising ease, lifted the massive log enough for the snake to slither free.

The serpent uncoiled itself slowly, its emerald scales glimmering in the dappled sunlight. Amelia expected gratitude, a sense of relief from the creature she'd rescued. But instead, the snake raised its head, its yellow eyes narrowed, and lunged at her. Amelia barely had time to jump back, her heart hammering against her ribs.

"Whoa, what was that for?" she exclaimed, adrenaline coursing through her veins. "I just helped you!"

The snake, a creature with a lifespan measured in decades, held no concept of human kindness or altruism. It saw Amelia as a potential threat, one it was now free to eliminate. Backing away slowly, Amelia scanned the jungle floor for an escape route.

"There has to be someone who can understand you," she muttered, desperately searching for a solution. Remembering a local legend about the wise woman of the forest, Amelia had an idea. "The village elder, maybe she can reason with you."

Amelia sprinted towards the distant sound of drumming; the rhythmic beat was a beacon of hope in the dense jungle. Reaching the clearing, she collapsed at the feet of Mama Abeni, the village elder, a woman whose wisdom was as revered as the ancient baobab trees.

Panting, Amelia explained the situation, the danger posed by the giant snake and its unexpected aggression. Mama Abeni listened patiently, her face an unreadable mask. Finally, she spoke, her voice raspy with age.

"The spirits of the forest act in ways we cannot always understand," she said, her gaze flickering to the edge of the clearing where the glint of emerald scales could be seen. "But sometimes, we can learn from their actions."

Without further explanation, Mama Abeni led Amelia back towards the fallen log. The snake had now coiled itself up into a slumber. Following Mama Abeni's instructions, Amelia carefully re-positioned the log, pinning the massive serpent once more.

For a moment, there was stunned silence. Then, the giant snake let out a guttural hiss of frustration, its struggles proving futile. It glared at Amelia, its cold eyes filled with defiance.

Mama Abeni placed a wrinkled hand on Amelia's shoulder. "It is not kindness that this creature understands," she said, "but consequences. Now, it will have time to reflect on its actions, trapped by the very thing it sought to escape."

As they left the clearing, Amelia glanced back at the pinned serpent. There was no gratitude, no regret, just a simmering anger. Yet, Amelia understood the lesson. Sometimes, kindness wasn't rewarded, and some things, like the nature of some creatures, couldn't be changed. Still, she had acted with compassion, a principle she wouldn't forsake.

The encounter left a lasting impression on Amelia. It wasn't just about the enigmatic serpent but about the delicate balance of the natural world. Sometimes, human intervention, even with the best intentions, could have unintended consequences. Amelia returned to her research, forever changed by the experience, forever carrying the memory of the emerald serpent, a testament to the unpredictable nature of the wild and the world at large.

THE RAINBOW

Based on the Zulu story about how
the rainbow was created.

According to Zulu mythology, the goddess
Unkulunkulu created the first man and woman,
and their tears mixed with the soil to create the first
rainbow. The rainbow serpent, known as Inkanyamba,
is revered as a symbol of creation and fertility.

The year is 2077. Once a bustling metropolis, Johannesburg is a skeleton of its former self. Towering chrome and glass buildings with reflective surfaces forever clouded by a perpetual dust storm. Rain, a forgotten memory, is a myth whispered by elders whose weathered faces mirrored the cracked earth. Water was the new gold, rationed and strictly controlled by the megacorporation AmajCorp.

Ntombi, a young woman with eyes the colour of the fabled blue skies, scavenged the wasteland with her older brother, Themba. Their faces, masked by dust rags, were etched with a desperation born from years of thirst. Today, their search led them to the ruins of the National Museum, a crumbling monument to forgotten history.

Inside, sunlight streamed through broken windows, illuminating a faded mural. It depicted a scene of vibrant greens and blues, an alien world where water cascaded, and a shimmering arc stretched across the sky. Ntombi gasped, pointing at the mural.

"Themba, what is that?"

Themba squinted. "Looks like some kind of story. Back when the world wasn't... this."

Ntombi traced the image of a giant serpent, its scales shimmering with a hundred colours, rising from a sparkling lake. Below, a man and woman wept, their tears mingling with the earth. Unlike anything Ntombi had ever seen, a vibrant arc arched over them.

"What is it?" she whispered, mesmerized.

Themba shrugged. "Legends, maybe. Before the Great Drying."

Ntombi's mind raced. Legends. Could the answer to their plight lie in forgotten stories? She spent the next few days devouring dusty scrolls and brittle tablets. Finally, she stumbled upon a text about Unkulunkulu, the creator, and the rainbow serpent, Inkanyamba. Hope, a fragile flower in the wasteland, bloomed in her chest.

That night, under the dim glow of scavenged batteries, Ntombi shared her discovery with Themba. "The rainbow serpent controls water! We have to find it!"

Themba was sceptical. "Legends are for storytellers, Ntombi. We need a real plan, not some mythical creature."

"But what other plan do we have? AmajCorp rations barely keep us alive. We're dying, Themba."

The desperation in her voice broke through his resistance. He sighed. "Alright, alright. But where do we even start?"

Ntombi pointed to a faded map. "The legend says Inkanyamba lives in the belly of the world, in a place called uMngeni."

uMngeni. The name sparked a memory in Themba. "There's an old tunnel network under the city leading to an abandoned water treatment plant. Maybe that's it?"

A spark of hope ignited in Ntombi's eyes. "We have to try."

The journey through the labyrinthine tunnels was treacherous. The air hung heavy with the smell of mould and decay. Broken pipes gurgled with stagnant water, the only liquid they'd encountered in weeks. Finally, they emerged into a vast cavern, unlike anything they'd ever seen.

Glowing crystals, remnants of a forgotten technology, cast an ethereal light, revealing a vast artificial lake. A magnificent serpent lay in its centre, coiled upon a crystalline platform. Its scales shimmered with every colour imaginable, and its eyes, pools of molten gold, fixed upon them.

Ntombi felt a primal fear course through her, but she pushed forward, dropping to her knees. "Great Inkanyamba," she pleaded, her voice hoarse, "we beg for your mercy. Our land is parched. Our people are dying. Please, share your water with us."

The serpent remained unmoving, its gaze unwavering. Ntombi felt a surge of despair. The legend had been a lie.

Suddenly, Themba stumbled, falling to his knees. "Ntombi," he rasped, clutching his stomach. The water deprivation had finally taken its toll.

Tears welled up in Ntombi's eyes. She looked up at the indifferent serpent, her voice breaking. "Please," she choked out, "help my brother. He doesn't have much time left."

And then, something remarkable happened. A single tear rolled down the serpent's golden eye, splashing into the lake. It sent ripples across the surface, and a column of water erupted from the centre. It was unlike any water they'd ever seen. It shimmered with an otherworldly light, vibrant and alive.

Ntombi rushed to Themba, cupping her hands and catching the cascading water. She forced it down his dry throat. He coughed, sputtering, then looked at her with newfound strength. Hope rekindled in his eyes.

Inkanyamba watched them, its gaze softening. With a low rumble that echoed through the cavern, the serpent spoke. Its voice was a symphony of rushing water and clinking crystals. "You have shown courage and compassion, little ones. You understand the true value of water, not just for survival, but for life itself."

Ntombi and Themba exchanged bewildered glances. The serpent could talk? "AmajCorp has twisted the flow of life," the serpent continued, its voice laced with sadness. "They hoard water for greed, not for the good of all."

Understanding dawned on Ntombi. "They're the reason the rain stopped! They control the water supply!"

"Indeed," the serpent rumbled. "But remember, child, water cannot be controlled. It can only be guided."

With a flick of its tail, the serpent created a smaller pool at the edge of the lake. The water shimmered, an echo of the larger pool. "Take this," the serpent boomed. "This water holds the memory of the life force. Use it wisely. Share it with your people. Plant the seeds of hope."

Ntombi and Themba filled every container they had brought. Though the weight was significant, it felt insignificant compared to the hope it carried. They bowed their heads in gratitude.

"Thank you, Inkanyamba," Ntombi whispered, tears glistening on her dust-streaked cheeks.

The serpent dipped its head in acknowledgement. "Remember, little ones, the true rainbow is not just in the sky but in the hearts of those who share."

The journey back was arduous, but their steps were lighter. They emerged from the tunnels, blinking in the harsh sunlight, the precious water carefully guarded.

Back in their shantytown, news of their discovery spread like wildfire. People gathered, their faces etched with disbelief and a flicker of hope. Ntombi and Themba shared the water, a single drop at a time. It was a meagre offering, but it was a start.

The water wasn't just water. It was a catalyst. As they shared it, they told the story of Inkanyamba, the serpent who reminded them of the true value of water. Inspired by the legend, people began to work together. They repaired old water collection systems, planted drought-resistant crops, and, most importantly, shared every drop they could spare.

The road to recovery was long and arduous. AmajCorp remained a constant threat, but a new spirit bloomed in the wasteland. People, united by the memory of the rainbow serpent and the power of shared resources, began to rebuild their lives.

Years later, a single tear rolled down her cheek as Ntombi stood overlooking a field of green shoots pushing through the cracked earth. It wasn't a tear of despair but a tear of hope. In the distance, a faint shimmer appeared in the sky, a promise whispered on the wind. It was the first sign of rain in decades, a fragile rainbow arcing across the horizon. The legend of Inkanyamba, a reminder of the power of compassion and the true value of water, had begun to rewrite their story.

THE TOKOLOSHE

Based on the African legend of the Tokoloshe.

The Tokoloshe is a mischievous, supernatural creature in South African folklore, feared for its pranks and vicious actions. It's said to be summoned by those with ill intentions, but there are rituals to protect against it. This myth is a cautionary tale about respecting the supernatural and not abusing its powers

The rhythmic chanting echoed through the dusty Johannesburg backstreets, punctuated by the pungent scent of burning herbs. Mpho, a young man with desperation etched on his face, stood at the centre of the ritual circle, his eyes pleading with Sangoma Gogo, the powerful healer.

"I need a quick rise, Gogo," Mpho rasped, his voice raw. "My business is failing, the loan sharks are circling, and my family …" His voice choked with emotion.

Gogo, her face a mask of wrinkles, studied him with obsidian eyes. "The Tokoloshe," she said, her voice a low growl, "is a creature of chaos, not fortune. He can bring ruin as easily as riches."

Mpho's shoulders slumped. He'd heard the whispers – the Tokoloshe, a hairy, goblin-like creature, could grant wishes, but at a terrible price. Yet, with his back against the wall, Mpho was drawn to the dark allure.

Ignoring Gogo's warnings, Mpho performed the forbidden ritual, offering blood and muttered incantations under a waning moon. Days later, a figure emerged from the shadows of an abandoned warehouse – the Tokoloshe. Small, grotesque, and with eyes glowing like embers, it cackled with glee.

"You have summoned me, mortal," it rasped, its voice like nails scraping on a chalkboard. "What is your desire?"

Mpho, fear mingling with desperation, choked out his wish – financial success. The Tokoloshe grinned, revealing needle-like teeth. "Your wish is granted," it hissed, "but remember, everything has a cost."

The next day, Mpho woke to news of a rival businessman collapsing, his empire crumbling. A wave of unease washed over Mpho, but the influx of seemingly easy money drowned it out. Soon, Mpho was living a life of luxury – a flashy car, a sprawling mansion, an aloof wife dripping with diamonds.

Yet, a darkness lurked beneath the gilded surface. Mpho's family grew distant, his friends vanished, and an unsettling silence filled the vast mansion. He became suspicious, paranoid, and convinced everyone was after his newfound wealth. Sleep became a stranger, replaced by nightmares of the Tokoloshe's cackle.

One stormy night, the Tokoloshe reappeared. Mpho, thinner and haunted, pleaded for release. "More money, more power!" the Tokoloshe mocked, its voice laced with sadistic glee. Realizing the trap he'd set for himself, Mpho understood the cost of his wish.

Desperate, he sought out Gogo. The old woman, her face grim, instructed him on a complex reversal ritual – an apology to the spirit world, acts of charity, and a return to his honest life. It was a long, arduous path, but Mpho, with newfound humility, persevered.

Slowly, things began to change. He sold

the mansion, downsized his business, and reconnected with his estranged family. The money dwindled, but a sense of peace, long forgotten, returned. One day, after a particularly kind act of charity, a feeling of lightness settled over him. He looked up, and for a fleeting moment, he saw a faint shimmer, a distorted image of the Tokoloshe, its face contorted in rage before it vanished.

Mpho knew then that he was finally free. He'd learned a harsh lesson – the Tokoloshe was a force of chaos, not creation. True success came from hard work, honesty, and respect for the natural order, including the unseen world. His story became a cautionary tale, a reminder that the supernatural, though powerful, was not to be trifled with. It was a force to be respected, not exploited, and balance, not greed, held the key to a fulfilling life.

THE HAUNTING OF CAPTAIN BART

Based on the African legend The Flying Dutchman.

This maritime legend is well-known worldwide but has a strong connection to the Cape of Good Hope in South Africa. It tells the story of a ghost ship cursed to sail the seas forever, representing the souls of sailors who died at sea. The Flying Dutchman is a significant part of South African maritime history and folklore.

The salty spray kissed Violet's freckled cheeks as she squinted out at the stormy horizon. Cape Town, a bustling port city at the tip of Africa, was a world away now, swallowed by the relentless churning of the South Atlantic. Beside her, Captain Bartholomew "Black Bart" Roberts, the notorious pirate, surveyed the tempest with an unsettling calm. Violet wasn't a pirate by choice. A stowaway aboard Black Bart's ship, the "Queen's Fury," she was trapped in a tempestuous situation, both literal and figurative.

"Land ahoy!" bellowed the lookout, his voice barely audible over the howling wind. Violet's heart lurched. This was the fabled Cape of Good Hope, the sailors' graveyard. Legends whispered of towering waves, treacherous currents, and the chilling presence of the Flying Dutchman, a ghostly ship doomed to sail the seas forever. Black Bart, however, seemed unfazed. "Prepare to weather the storm, lads!" he roared, his voice tinged with a thrill that sent shivers down Violet's spine.

The storm arrived with a vengeance. Towering waves, the colour of angry pewter, slammed against the "Queen's Fury," threatening to swallow it whole. The ship, creaking and groaning under the strain, danced a precarious jig on the turbulent surface. Violet clung to the railing, her knuckles white, her heart pounding a frantic rhythm against her ribs. Around her, the seasoned pirates, their faces etched with a grim determination born from countless storms, wrestled with the sails and lines, battling to keep the ship afloat.

Then, amidst the deafening roar of the wind and the crashing waves, a spectral outline emerged from the swirling mist. A colossal ship, its sails tattered and black, materialized, casting an unnatural chill over the "Queen's Fury." The air crackled with an unseen energy, and the sailors murmured amongst themselves, their faces pale with fear. "The Flying Dutchman!" a young sailor shrieked, dropping his rigging tools with a clatter. Black Bart, however, remained uncowed. He barked orders, his voice a defiant challenge to the spectral vessel.

The storm intensified as if responding to the confrontation. Waves crashed against the "Queen's Fury" with bone-crushing force, threatening to split the timbers. Violet felt a wave of nausea rise in her throat, but she forced it down, her gaze riveted on the spectral ship. Suddenly, a figure materialized on the deck of the Flying Dutchman. Tall and shrouded in an ethereal glow, it beckoned Black Bart towards it. Violet gasped, her breath catching in her throat.

Black Bart, his own face grim and resolute, met the spectral figure's gaze. A tense silence stretched, punctuated only by the howling wind and the creaking of the ships. Then, in a voice that seemed to echo from the depths of the sea itself, the figure spoke. Its words were in a language Violet didn't understand, yet their meaning was chillingly clear. It was a challenge, an offer of some sort, a dark bargain perhaps.

Black Bart's response was a guttural laugh that boomed across the storm-wracked sea. He raised a tankard of rum high, a defiant toast to the spectral figure and the cursed ship. The figure on the Flying Dutchman seemed to shimmer in rage before vanishing as abruptly as it had appeared.

The storm, as if mirroring the confrontation, began to wane. The spectral outline of the Flying Dutchman faded into the mist, leaving behind an eerie silence. Black Bart, his face etched with a grim determination Violet hadn't seen before, barked orders, steering the "Queen's Fury" away from the Cape.

The encounter left an indelible mark on Violet. Black Bart became uncharacteristically withdrawn, his eyes haunted by a new depth. He spoke little of the ghostly encounter, but a coldness seemed to have settled within him. He still led the "Queen's Fury" on daring raids, his thirst for plunder seemingly undimmed, but a shadow of fear now followed them. The once boisterous evenings were filled with an unsettling silence, broken only by the clinking of tankards and the murmur of nervous conversations.

One night, under the cloak of darkness, Violet overheard a hushed conversation between two senior officers. They spoke of a dark pact, a price Black Bart had paid to escape the clutches of the Flying Dutchman. The details were sketchy, whispers of an ancient artefact Black Bart had stolen and was now bound to retrieve for the cursed vessel. Fear gnawed at Violet. This wasn't just about Black Bart's fear – it was about their own survival. If Black Bart failed to deliver the artefact, what would become of them?

Several months later, during a daring raid on a Spanish galleon, Violet saw her opportunity. The chaos of the battle provided the perfect cover. She slipped away, making her way to a small boat hidden amongst the reeds. As the "Queen's Fury" sailed away, laden with plundered treasures, Violet rowed with all her might, the image of the spectral Dutchman a constant reminder in her mind. The journey was long and perilous. Weeks turned into months as she battled treacherous currents and navigated by the stars. Hunger gnawed at her, and thirst parched her throat. Yet, the fear of Black Bart and the unknown fate that awaited them on the "Queen's Fury" fuelled her determination.

Finally, a smudge on the horizon resolved itself

into the familiar silhouette of Tortuga, a notorious pirate haven. Relief washed over Violet as she steered the boat towards the bustling harbour. Here, amidst the taverns overflowing with rum and the streets teeming with pirates of all stripes, she might find answers and perhaps even allies.

Days turned into weeks as Violet weaved her way through the labyrinthine alleys of Tortuga, piecing together rumours and whispers about Black Bart and his recent exploits. The stories were fragmented and often embellished, but a common thread emerged. Black Bart was indeed searching for an artefact, an ancient amulet rumoured to hold immense power, hidden somewhere in the jungles of a forgotten Mayan temple.

One evening, in a smoke-filled tavern reeking of stale ale and sweat, Violet stumbled upon a weathered old sailor with a face etched with the stories of a thousand storms. He was regaling a group with a tale. The old sailor spoke of a pirate captain, once fearless, who had defied the Flying Dutchman at the Cape of Good Hope. He said the captain was a changed man, haunted by unseen forces, searching for a mythical amulet to appease the cursed ship.

The other pirates scoffed, dismissing the story as mere superstition. But for Violet, it was a revelation. This sailor was talking about Black Bart, and the details of his story, particularly the mention of the amulet, resonated with the whispers she had gathered. But something didn't quite add up. If Black Bart had defied the Flying Dutchman, why was he haunted? The legend spoke of a cursed ship, not a cursed captain.

Leaving the tavern, Violet pondered the mystery. The encounter at the Cape, the spectral figure's words in that unknown tongue, and Black Bart's newfound fear remained a chilling puzzle. As the moon cast its silvery light on the choppy waters of the harbour, Violet knew she couldn't ignore it. Black Bart might be a ruthless pirate, but the "Queen's Fury" crew were innocent men, and she wouldn't abandon them to their fate.

Fuelled by a newfound purpose, Violet decided to take matters into her own hands. She would find the amulet before Black Bart and use it to break whatever dark pact he had made with the Flying Dutchman. It was a dangerous gamble, but it was her only hope of saving herself and the crew. The next morning, with a map gleaned from a drunken pirate and a heart full of trepidation, Violet set sail once more, this time not away from danger, but towards it, into the heart of the uncharted jungle, on a desperate quest for a mythical amulet and the redemption of a ruthless pirate.

THE GROOTSLANG

Based on the African legend of The Grootslang.

A creature born of a divine mistake, the Grootslang
is a legendary monster believed to inhabit a cave
in the Richtersveld region. It's said to be a massive
serpent with an elephant's head, known for its
cunning and strength. This myth has inspired
countless tales and adventures throughout history.

Dr Zahara "Zee" Patel squinted at the satellite image, her brow furrowed. The Richtersveld, a seemingly endless stretch of rugged South African terrain, revealed an anomaly. A circular depression, perfectly round and unlike any natural erosion pattern Zee had ever seen. It was almost … unnatural.

Zee was a geologist, not a mythologist, but the legend of the Grootslang, the giant elephant-headed serpent, had always held a strange fascination for her. Local folklore spoke of a hidden cavern, guarded by the Grootslang, overflowing with diamonds. While Zee dismissed the creature itself as a fanciful invention, the idea of an undiscovered geological wonder piqued her scientific curiosity.

Funding the expedition was a challenge. Investors scoffed at the idea, calling it a wild goose chase. But Zee, fuelled by a blend of scientific ambition and a touch of childhood wonder, finally secured a grant from a quirky billionaire with a penchant for the unusual.

The journey to the Richtersveld was arduous. The team consisted of Zee, her gruff but reliable field guide, Khoza, and a young, enthusiastic geologist named Leo. Reaching the anomaly took days of trekking under the relentless African sun.

The depression was vast, its edges impossibly smooth. Khoza, a man steeped in local lore, cast a wary glance around. "The Grootslang," he muttered, his voice laced with a healthy dose of trepidation. Zee scoffed good-naturedly. "Don't worry, Khoza. We're not here for diamonds, just a good rock sample."

Setting up camp, Zee spent days studying the depression. It behaved unlike any known geological formation. Readings were erratic, hinting at something … alien. One particularly stormy night, a crack echoed across the valley. Following the sound, they discovered a fissure at the base of the depression.

Hesitantly, Zee peered into the darkness. A cold gust of air tickled her nose, carrying with it the faintest whisper. It wasn't a sound but a feeling, a sense of ancient power emanating from the depths. Khoza tensed beside her. "The Grootslang," he mumbled again, his voice barely a whisper.

Fear warred with scientific curiosity within Zee. This was an opportunity for a groundbreaking discovery, a chance to rewrite textbooks. Yet, a primal part of her recoiled from the unknown. Taking a deep breath, Zee equipped herself with a high-powered flashlight and a healthy dose of scepticism.

The descent into the cavern was a claustrophobic nightmare. The air grew thick and humid, and the rock walls dripped with unnatural condensation. Finally, they reached a vast chamber illuminated by an otherworldly glow emanating from ... a giant egg.

It pulsed with an inner light, shimmering like a giant opal. Zee, her mind reeling, approached cautiously. It felt warm, almost alive. As she reached out, a crack appeared on the egg's surface.

A low rumble echoed through the cavern, making the earth tremble.

Panic seized Zee. This wasn't a creature of myth but something far more primal, a force of nature awakened by their intrusion. Scrambling back, Zee tripped, landing hard on the cavern floor. Looking up, she met the gaze of two enormous, intelligent eyes.

The Grootslang wasn't a creature of local legend but something far older, a geological entity slumbering deep within the earth. Its form, a combination of mineral deposits and bioluminescent organisms, bore a passing resemblance to the local myth.

The Grootslang didn't attack, but its gaze held a silent warning. Zee understood. They had violated an ancient serenity, awakened a force they weren't meant to disturb. The team scurried back to the surface, the cavern entrance mysteriously closing behind them.

Back at their camp, shaken but strangely exhilarated, Zee realized the true significance of their discovery. The Grootslang wasn't a monster but a testament to the earth's hidden wonders. Perhaps the legend passed down through generations had been a way for the people to understand and respect a power beyond human comprehension.

The expedition did not return with diamonds but with a discovery that would revolutionize the understanding of the earth's geological history. Zee's findings, a blend of scientific evidence and respect for local folklore, ignited a new era of collaborative research.

The story of the Grootslang, once a fantastical tale, became a bridge between myth and science, a reminder that the secrets of the earth are often stranger than fiction and that respecting the legends of the past might hold the key to unlocking the future.

THE WHITE LION

Based on the African story The
White Lion of Timbavati.

This legend tells of a group of South African
Shangaan people who believe white lions are sacred
and divine. They consider them to be messengers of
the gods and bringers of prosperity. White lions are
considered so precious that they have been the subject
of conservation efforts in the Timbavati region.

Anya, a young wildlife photographer, crouched
amongst the tall savanna grass, her heart
pounding in a frantic rhythm against her ribs.
Through the lens of her camera, she watched a
magnificent sight—a pride of lions led by a male
with a coat the colour of freshly fallen snow. This
wasn't just any lion; it was Duma, the legendary
white lion of the Timbavati.

For generations, the Shangaan people who lived on
the reserve's borders revered white lions. Duma,
born in defiance of genetics, was seen as a sacred
messenger, a symbol of good fortune. Anya, raised
on rational science, wasn't so sure. Yet, as she

witnessed Duma's calm leadership and effortless grace as he stalked prey, a flicker of something she couldn't explain ignited within her.

Anya's photos of Duma went viral, captivating the world. Fuelled by greed and a distorted sense of conquest, Trophy hunters started whispering about the "ghost lion." Anya, horrified, realized the unintended consequence of her work. Conservation efforts had always focused on protecting the more numerous tawny lions, but Duma was now in danger.

Driven by a newfound purpose, Anya joined forces with the Shangaan people. Together, they launched a campaign to educate the public about the sanctity of white lions, emphasizing their cultural significance. Anya's photos, once mere snapshots, became a powerful advocacy tool.

The fight wasn't easy. Trophy hunting lobbies pushed back, wielding money and influence. But Anya and the Shangaan people refused to back down. They organized protests, petitioned government officials, and used social media to amplify their message. Slowly, the tide began to turn.

Public opinion shifted. People saw the beauty of white lions not just as trophies but as living symbols of the natural world's wonder. Conservation efforts received a much-needed boost, with funding specifically directed towards protecting white lions.

One day, while on patrol, Anya encountered poachers setting up snares. They were armed, and fear coiled in her stomach. But then, she heard a low growl. Duma was emerging from the tall grass, his white coat starkly contrasting with the encroaching darkness. The poachers, seeing the legendary lion, fled in terror.

Duma stood guard for a while before disappearing back into the savanna. Anya knew then that Duma wasn't just a symbol; he was a guardian, a protector of his land and its creatures. The respect she once lacked had blossomed into a deep reverence.

Duma lived a long life, a living testament to the power of conservation and cultural understanding. Anya continued her work, using her lens to show the world the beauty of nature, not just the spectacular but also the delicate balance that needed to be protected. The legend of the White Lion lived on, not as a mythical creature, but as a reminder that true prosperity comes from respecting the natural world and its sacred wonders.

THE DONKEY

Based on the legend of The Donkey
that Depicts Death.

In South African tradition, it's believed that if you hear a donkey braying in the night, it's a warning that a ghost is nearby. Donkeys are thought to have a spiritual connection, and their braying may indicate the presence of the supernatural.

Maya, a city girl on a summer internship at a remote wildlife sanctuary in South Africa, wasn't prepared for the eerie stillness of the nights. Here, the only sounds were unseen creatures' rustling and nocturnal insects' chirping. Then, one night, a heart-stopping bray shattered the silence.

It wasn't the comforting nicker of a horse; it was a long, mournful sound that seemed to echo through the star-studded sky. Maya shot upright in her bunk, her heart hammering against her ribs. Goosebumps erupted on her skin as she listened for a repeat, but all was quiet.

In the following days, Maya learned about the local legend – a donkey's bray at night meant a ghost was nearby. The older workers spoke of it with a mixture of respect and trepidation. Maya, a self-proclaimed pragmatist, dismissed it as superstition. Still, the memory of that chilling bray lingered.

One particularly hot afternoon, while exploring a seldom-used reserve section, Maya stumbled upon a dilapidated barn. Curiosity piqued, she pushed open the creaking door, a wave of dust swirling within. A rusted cart stood in the centre, and in the dim light, Maya saw ... a donkey.

But this wasn't any ordinary donkey. Its coat was a dusty grey, its eyes dull and lifeless. It stood frozen, emanating a sense of despair. Maya felt a pang of sympathy, a sense of something unfinished about the creature.

Over the next few days, Maya found herself drawn back to the barn. She'd leave a bucket of fresh water and a handful of hay, her heart clenching as the creature approached hesitantly. The donkey seemed tethered to the barn, unable to leave.

One night, the familiar heart-stopping bray echoed through the reserve. Panic surged through Maya, but something was different this time. The sound wasn't coming from a distance but from within the barn itself.

Armed with a flashlight, Maya raced towards the sound. The ghostly donkey was rearing in distress in the barn, its mournful bray intensifying. It seemed trapped, an invisible barrier keeping it from leaving the stall.

Suddenly, it hit Maya. This wasn't a ghost but a neglected, tethered animal; it bray, a desperate cry for help. She traced the rope to a rusted post outside the barn, the tether long since snapped. The donkey wasn't tethered anymore but was bound by fear and the memory of its confinement.

With gentle coaxing, Maya managed to lead the donkey out of the barn. It took days, but with patience and care, Maya helped the donkey regain its trust. One morning, she found the stall empty – the donkey, finally free, had disappeared.

The mournful bray never returned. Maya never saw the donkey again, but she knew it was free.

And perhaps, in her own way, Maya had helped a restless spirit find solace, turning a local legend into a story of compassion and understanding.

OR, PERHAPS YOU WOULD PREFER THIS MORE CHILLING ENDING …

Maya shivered, the memory of the unearthly bray clinging to her like the dust from the abandoned barn. Ignoring the prickle of unease, she trudged back to the wildlife sanctuary, the setting sun casting long shadows across the parched earth. Days blurred into weeks, the silence punctuated only by the rhythmic chirping of unseen insects and the constant, nagging worry about the ghostly donkey.

One afternoon, a ranger named Sabelo, a weathered man steeped in local lore, noticed Maya lingering near the deserted barn. He approached cautiously. "Looking for the Lost One, are you?" His voice was a low rumble.

Maya hesitated. "The Lost One?"

"The donkey," Sabelo explained. "They say its bray is a harbinger of death. Some say it's the restless spirit of a farmhand, wronged by his master and condemned to wander the earth as a donkey forever."

A shiver ran down Maya's spine. The legend suddenly felt less like a bedtime story and more like a chilling prophecy. The haunting bray had coincided with her arrival at the sanctuary, and now, an unsettling sense of foreboding gnawed at her.

Days turned into a relentless cycle of fear and fascination. Maya continued to leave food and water, determined to help the spectral donkey, even if it meant defying the legend. The wind howled like a banshee one stormy night, rattling the sanctuary's windows. That night, the bray returned, closer this time, filled with a raw desperation.

Ignoring the pleas of the other interns, Maya raced towards the barn, flashlight slicing through the darkness. Inside, the ghostly donkey thrashed against an invisible barrier, eyes filled with a terrifying panic. But this time, something was different. The barn felt colder, the air thick with an unnatural energy.

As Maya edged closer, the donkey let out

a deafening shriek, its form shimmering and distorting. Panic seized Maya, a sense of overwhelming dread threatening to consume her. She stumbled backwards, tripping over a loose floorboard. The flashlight clattered to the ground, plunging her into darkness.

A bloodcurdling bray filled the air, followed by an unearthly silence. When the storm subsided the next morning, it revealed Maya crumpled on the barn floor, still clutching the snapped tethered rope. The search party found no sign of the ghostly donkey, only an unsettling peace hanging heavy in the air.

News of Maya's death spread through the reserve like wildfire. Sabelo, his face etched with grief, addressed the interns. "Sometimes," he said, his voice heavy, "helping those bound by tragedy comes at a cost. The Lost One found peace, but perhaps it took a life to grant it."

The legend of the ghostly donkey lingered, a cautionary tale whispered around campfires. The barn stood silent, a stark reminder of the tragedy that unfolded within its walls. Maya's death confirmed the villagers' worst fears – the donkey's bray wasn't just a harbinger of death; it was the cause. But was it the death of the wronged farmhand seeking vengeance or the price of disturbing a restless spirit seeking solace? The answer remained shrouded in the mystery of the Lost One, a chilling testament to the blurred lines between legend and reality.

THE PROTECTOR

Based on the Zulu Legend of Umlindi Wemingizimu.

This Zulu legend tells the story of a great protector of the Southern African region, Umlindi Wemingizimu. As the guardian of the south, he ensures the well-being of the land and its inhabitants. This myth highlights the spiritual connection between the land and its people.

The year is 2079. Cape Town, once a vibrant coastal city, now resembled a forgotten film set. Towering skyscrapers, once gleaming testaments to human ambition, stood like hollow teeth against a perpetually blood-red sky. The Great Drying, a merciless drought fuelled by climate change, had choked the life out of the land, leaving behind a wasteland ruled by dust and desperation.

Anya, a young woman with eyes the colour of faded turquoise, scavenged the ruins with her grandmother, Gogo. Gogo, weathered and wise with years etched into her face like intricate maps, moved slower these days. Yet, her spirit remained untamed, fuelled by a flicker of defiance and a love for the land that ran deeper than any dry riverbed.

"Look, Anya," Gogo rasped, pointing towards a shimmering object partially buried in the sand.

Anya squinted through the dust storm and saw a fragmented clay tablet adorned with strange symbols. Carefully, she brushed away the sand, revealing intricate patterns that seemed to dance and flow.

Back in their makeshift shelter, a rickety tent cobbled together from salvaged materials, Gogo lit a flickering candle and traced the symbols on the tablet. "These markings," she whispered, "they speak of Umlindi Wemingizimu, the Great Southern Guardian."

Anya's eyes widened. Legends, mostly dismissed as bedtime stories in a world struggling for survival, were suddenly filled with a glimmer of hope. "The one who protects the land?" she asked, her voice hushed with awe.

Gogo nodded. "The stories say he can call the rain, bring life back to the parched earth. But..." her voice trailed off, a heavy silence filling the air.

"But what, Gogo?"

"He sleeps now," Gogo continued, her voice filled with sorrow. "The disrespect for the land and the endless greed of corporations like AmajCorp have weakened his spirit."

A spark ignited in Anya's heart. If Umlindi Wemingizimu was the answer, then they had to awaken him. But how? Anya spent the next few days devouring dusty scrolls and brittle tablets found in abandoned libraries. Days turned into weeks, the knowledge gleaned, filling her with hope and a daunting sense of responsibility.

An ancient ritual emerged – a ceremony requiring a specific plant, the Imphepho, known for its resilience in dry conditions. Anya knew finding it would be a long shot, but it was their only hope.

Their journey took them across the cracked earth, the unforgiving sun beating down on their backs. Days blurred into one another, punctuated only by the relentless wind and the gnawing hunger. Just as hope began to dwindle, a miracle unfolded. In a small crevice between two parched rocks, a stubborn little plant sprouted – a single stalk of

Imphepho, its leaves a vibrant green that defied the surrounding desolation.

Anya felt a surge of joy as she carefully dug up the plant, cradling it like a precious jewel. With renewed vigour, they pushed on, guided by fragmented stories about a hidden cave said to be a gateway to Umlindi Wemingizimu.

Finally, after weeks of relentless searching, they found it – a gaping maw carved into the side of a mountain, shrouded in perpetual twilight. Gogo held Anya back, her hand trembling.

"Be careful, child," she warned. "The paths of the spirits are not meant for mortal feet."

But Anya was resolute. With a deep breath, she stepped into the cave, the cool darkness enveloping her. She walked for what felt like an eternity, the air thick with an ancient energy. Finally, she emerged into a cavern bathed in an ethereal glow.

In the centre stood a colossal figure, its form shifting and swirling like a sandstorm. It was Umlindi Wemingizimu, the Great Southern Guardian. However, this wasn't the majestic protector she imagined. He appeared faded, his form flickering like an almost extinguished flame.

Anya knelt before him, clutching the Imphepho. "Great Guardian," she pleaded, her voice trembling, "our land is dying. AmajCorp controls the water, treating it as a commodity, not a life source. We need your help."

Silence. Umlindi Wemingizimu seemed unmoving, his eyes pools of swirling dust, reflecting the desolation of the land they'd left behind. Anya felt a wave of despair, but a single tear rolled down the Guardian's face. It landed at Anya's feet, not a tear of water, but a single glistening grain of sand.

"Your connection to the land is broken," rumbled a voice that echoed through the cavern. "You treat it as a commodity, not a living entity. As long as that continues, I remain weak."

Unyielding, Anya raised her head, holding the Imphepho aloft. "We understand now, Great Guardian. We've treated the land with disrespect. But it's not too late. We can learn to respect it again, to nurture it back to health. We can show you that we deserve your protection."

Anya's words, imbued with sincerity and desperation, seemed to flicker a spark in Umlindi Wemingizimu's eyes. From within the dust storm that formed his body, a small, luminous green orb emerged, pulsing with a gentle light. It floated towards the Imphepho, merging with the resilient plant in a soft glow.

"This is the seed of life," rumbled the Guardian's voice, softer now, less filled with despair. "Plant it in the heart of your land. Care for it, and nurture it with your respect and newfound knowledge. If the land responds, and the seed grows, then my spirit will awaken once more."

Anya clutched the glowing Imphepho, a newfound purpose burning in her heart. She knew the road ahead wouldn't be easy. AmajCorp was a powerful entity, and their greed was an ever-present threat. But now, she wasn't alone. She had Gogo, the knowledge of her ancestors, and the seed of hope – a symbol of a renewed relationship with the land.

The journey back was arduous but filled with a renewed sense of purpose. Back in their makeshift shelter, Anya, guided by ancient texts, prepared the ground. With Gogo by her side, she planted the glowing Imphepho, a lone beacon of hope in the desolate landscape.

Days turned into weeks, then months. The harsh sun beat down, and the wind howled, but Anya and Gogo tended to the plant with unwavering devotion. Anya would pour what little water they had on the soil every morning, praying for a sign.

Just as doubt began to creep in, a miracle happened. One morning, a tiny green shoot emerged from the ground, pushing its way through the dust. Anya gasped, tears welling in her eyes. It was a small victory, but a victory, nonetheless.

News of the "magic plant" spread like wildfire through the parched communities around Cape Town. People, desperate for hope, flocked to see the miracle. Inspired by Anya's dedication and the knowledge passed down by Gogo, they began to learn forgotten practices of rainwater harvesting, soil conservation, and sustainable farming.

A wave of change swept through the wasteland. Communities came together, sharing resources and knowledge. Anya became a symbol of their fight, the young woman who dared to reawaken the spirit of the land.

This did not go unnoticed by AmajCorp. They saw their control over water resources slipping through their fingers. One night, disguised figures raided Anya and Gogo's shelter, stealing the glowing Imphepho.

Anya and Gogo were devastated, but they wouldn't give up. Anya rallied the communities, a newfound strength in her voice. They knew where AmajCorp's headquarters were – a towering chrome monolith in the heart of the city.

Together, they marched on the headquarters, thousands strong, armed not with weapons but with shovels, hoes, and buckets. They chanted slogans about respect for the land and the power of unity.

The march surprised AmajCorp's security. The sheer number of people overwhelmed them. Inside the building, chaos erupted. As the crowd surged forward, a security guard accidentally knocked over a highly flammable container, causing the building to go up in flames.

In the ensuing confusion, Anya managed to retrieve the glowing Imphepho. As she emerged from the burning building, she looked towards the sky, a vast expanse painted in shades of orange and red by the fire. Then, something miraculous happened.

A single dark cloud appeared on the horizon, growing larger with each passing moment. A low rumble echoed through the air, followed by the first drops of rain in years.

The crowd erupted in cheers, falling to their knees and crying tears of joy. As the rain fell, washing away the dust and ash, a faint green glow emanated from the Imphepho in Anya's hand.

High above, in the heart of the storm, a colossal figure materialized, its form swirling with rain and mist. Umlindi Wemingizimu, the Great Southern Guardian, was awake once more, his spirit revitalized by the bond between the land and its people.

The rain continued for days, replenishing the parched earth and bringing life back to the wasteland. AmajCorp's control over water was shattered. People learned to live in harmony with the land again, nurturing it with respect and knowledge passed down through generations.

Years later, Anya stood amidst a field of thriving crops, a vibrant green tapestry replacing the wasteland of her childhood. Gogo, although older now, smiled with a profound sense of accomplishment. In the distance, a shimmering rainbow arched across the sky, a testament to their resilience and renewed connection with Umlindi Wemingizimu. The legend of the Great Southern Guardian had become a living reality, a reminder that even in the face of immense adversity, hope, like a tiny seed, could blossom into a powerful force for change.

However, the victory wasn't without its challenges. AmajCorp, though weakened, still existed, their greed simmering beneath the surface. Anya knew their fight was far from over. With Gogo by her side, she turned to the young people who had grown up under the renewed rain, their eyes sparkling with curiosity.

"This land is in your hands now," Anya declared, holding up the Imphepho, its glow now a permanent fixture. "The stories of Umlindi Wemingizimu and the lessons learned from the Great Drying, pass them on. Never forget the importance of respect for the earth, for it sustains us all."

The young people, their faces filled with determination, took up shovels and saplings, their laughter echoing across the land. Anya watched them, a sense of pride swelling in her chest. The future, once uncertain, now shimmered with the promise of a thriving land protected by a people who understood its true value. As she looked towards the Drakensberg Mountains, a faint outline of the colossal figure could be seen against the horizon, a silent guardian forever bound to the land and its people.

THE TRICKSTER HARE

Based on the African legend of Orion
and the Trickster Hare.

In several South African cultures, the constellation Orion is associated with various myths and stories. The San people, for example, have tales of Orion as a hunter, and in some versions, he is tricked by the hare. These stories often explore themes of bravery, wisdom, and cunning.

The Cape Town night sky glittered, a million stars a stark contrast to the harsh neon glow of the taxi rank. Chike, muscles tight with exhaustion after a long shift at the docks, longed for the quiet of his Khayelitsha shack. He hailed a dented minibus, its paint job a kaleidoscope of faded glory.

As Chike squeezed into a cramped seat, a figure radiating nervous energy entered behind him. It was Khumba, the notorious "Hare." Khumba, a drug lord, was a man of nimble fingers and a silver tongue, unlike his namesake, notorious for outsmarting even the strongest contenders.

"Need a lift to Paradise, brother?" Khumba's voice oozed a false charm. The nickname "Paradise" for Khumba's territory was a cruel joke. Drugs and violence were its currency. Chike, wary but desperate to get home quickly, mumbled his destination.

The minibus weaved through the darkened streets, finally reaching a dusty crossroads. Khumba gestured for Chike to follow. "Shortcut," he said, a sly glint in his eyes.

Chicke hesitated. "Don't trust shortcuts with you, Khumba."

Khumba chuckled a high-pitched sound that grated on Chike's nerves. "Just follow the belt, my friend Orion's belt." He pointed at the constellation hanging low in the sky, the three bright stars a celestial landmark.

Chike knew the legend – in the San stories, Orion, the hunter, was often outsmarted by the cunning Hare. But surely, Khumba wouldn't …

Before Chike knew it, the driver was following the constellation. They traversed a maze of deserted alleyways, the air thick with the stench of garbage and decay. Chike's unease grew with each turn. Finally, they emerged into a clearing – Khumba's "Paradise."

Instead of a haven, it was a scene of chaos. Junkies sprawled on the ground, their eyes glazed over, their bodies ravaged. Dealers hawked their wares, their voices echoing in the desolate night.

Khumba's smile widened. "Welcome home, Chike. Seen you working hard, thought maybe you needed a … diversion." He gestured towards a table overflowing with drugs.

Chike's anger flared. He wasn't a fool. Khumba was trying to drag him into his web. "Nice try, Hare," Thembi spat. "But Orion ain't falling for your tricks."

Suddenly, a police siren wailed in the distance. Khumba's face contorted in fury. "Cops!" he yelled. The clearing erupted in chaos. Chike, using the confusion, sprinted back towards the main road, Khumba's enraged shouts echoing behind him.

He reached the crossroads, gasping for breath. Orion's belt, now high in the sky, seemed to wink at him, a celestial guide leading him home. He hailed another taxi, his heart pounding with a mixture of fear and defiance.

Chike might have been a simple dockworker, but tonight, he had outwitted the notorious Hare. The legend of Orion, a reminder of bravery and cunning, echoed in his ears as he finally reached his shack, the first rays of dawn painting the horizon. Chike might not have been a hunter, but tonight, he'd outsmarted a predator.

THE STAR CHASER

Based on the African legend about The Star Chasers of the San People.

The San people have stories about "star chasers" who pursue celestial animals in the night sky. These tales emphasize the San's deep connection with the cosmos and their interpretations of constellations.

The Kalahari night sky was a canvas ablaze with stars. Unlike the neon-drenched cities he'd grown up in, here, under the vast expanse of the Milky Way, Keletso felt a sense of belonging. Tonight, however, the stars weren't his focus. His keen eyes scanned the red dunes, searching for the tell-tale shimmer of a gemsbok herd.

Keletso, a young San man raised in a Johannesburg township, had returned to his ancestral land a year ago. His grandfather, Mxolisi, the last living San elder in their family, lay frail in their makeshift hut. Keletso yearned to understand the old ways, the stories whispered under starry nights, before it was all lost.

Tonight, under the watchful gaze of the Milky Way, he was hunting, not for trophies, but for his grandfather, who craved fresh springbok meat, a taste of his youth. Keletso gripped his bow, its wood smooth from generations of use, and followed the faint tracks in the sand.

Hours melted into the night. Just as fatigue began to gnaw at him, he spotted them – a herd of springbok, their graceful forms silhouetted against the moonlit dunes. Adrenaline surged through Keletso. He lowered himself to the ground, stalking closer with practised ease.

Suddenly, a streak of blue light pierced the night sky, arcing over the springbok. They scattered in panic, their hooves kicking up sand in a frenzy. Keletso stared in disbelief, his heart pounding against his ribs.

Where had that blinding light come from? It wasn't a shooting star – it moved too erratically. As his eyes adjusted, he saw it – a long, slender object hovering silently a few kilometres away. It emitted a faint blue glow, pulsing like a beating heart.

Curiosity overpowering his initial fear, Keletso

started towards the object. He moved cautiously, the silence broken only by the crunch of sand under his boots. As he neared, the object lowered itself, revealing a sleek, metallic craft, unlike anything he'd ever seen.

A hatch on the side opened with a hiss. A figure emerged, tall and slender, with skin that shimmered silver under the moonlight. It moved with an ethereal grace, its eyes two pools of deep blue light. Fear turned to awe as Keletso watched the being approach.

"Do not be afraid," the being spoke in a voice that resonated within his mind, not through his ears. "We come in peace."

Keletso found his voice dry and shaky. "Who are you? Where do you come from?"

"We are the Star Chasers," the being replied. "We travel the cosmos, following the celestial pathways, learning from the wisdom of the stars."

Keletso's mind raced. Star Chasers? Wasn't that a story from Mxolisi's tales – mythical beings who chased celestial animals across the Milky Way? Did his grandfather's stories hold a truth he hadn't understood?

"You know our stories?" he asked, a tremor of excitement in his voice.

The being smiled, a luminous blue light emanating from its face. "We exist within the stories, carried through generations by those who hold the stars in their hearts. You, a descendant of the San, are one such keeper."

Keletso felt a connection spark between them, a shared understanding of the ancient language of the stars. He poured out his story – his grandfather's failing health and the yearning to understand his roots. The Star Chaser listened patiently.

"Your grandfather," it finally said, "honoured the stars. His connection to the cosmos runs deep. Perhaps there is a way to help him."

The Star Chaser placed a hand on Keletso's shoulder, and a surge of energy coursed through him. Images flooded his mind – constellations swirling into existence, celestial creatures morphing into familiar animals. He understood.

"The springbok you seek," the Star Chaser continued, "is not just an animal. It represents the life force, the constellation of the Springbok in the sky. By respecting the animal, your grandfather honours the cosmos itself."

Keletso understood. He wasn't meant to hunt the springbok tonight. He needed to find another way.

The Star Chaser took a small, glowing orb from within its craft. "Take this," it said, handing it to Keletso. "It holds the essence of the springbok constellation. Place it near your grandfather. It may help rekindle his connection to the cosmos, to the life force that flows through everything."

With a final nod, the Star Chaser disappeared back into its craft. The light pulsed brighter, then dimmed, before the craft itself faded into the night, leaving behind only a faint shimmering trail in the sky.

Keletso stood there, the glowing orb warm in his hand, the encounter leaving him breathless. He returned to the village under the faint light of dawn, his mind reeling with the night's events. Reaching the hut, he found Mxolisi weak but awake, his eyes gazing at the fading stars.

"Mxolisi," Keletso whispered, kneeling beside him. "I have something for you." He explained his encounter with the Star Chasers, his voice hushed with awe. He hesitated, then placed the orb in his grandfather's frail hand.

Mxolisi's eyes widened. "The Springbok constellation," he rasped, his voice weak but filled with wonder. As his hand closed around the orb, a warm light pulsed through the hut, casting an ethereal glow on their faces.

Keletso watched, mesmerized, as a surge of energy seemed to flow through his grandfather. The lines on his face softened, a faint colour returning to his cheeks. Mxolisi took a deep breath, the first true breath Keletso had heard him take in days.

"The stories are true," Mxolisi whispered, his voice filled with a newfound strength. "The Star Chasers Walk among us. They guard the wisdom of the stars."

Keletso nodded, the encounter solidifying his belief in his heritage, in the stories he once dismissed as mere fables. He looked out the hut, the rising sun painting the sky with fiery hues.

Suddenly, a loud screech echoed through the village. Startled, Keletso and Mxolisi rushed out. There, in the centre of the settlement, lay a dead springbok. Hunters from a neighbouring village, known for their disregard for tradition and their ruthless hunting practices, stood over the carcass, their faces contorted in surprise.

Keletso felt a surge of anger fuelled by a sense of responsibility. He walked towards the hunters, the glowing orb of the Springbok constellation still warm in his pocket.

"This is a sacred land," he said, his voice firm. "You disrespect the life force, the spirit of the animal."

The leader of the other hunters, a burly man with a scarred face, scoffed. "There are no spirits here, boy. Just meat for the taking."

Keletso stepped forward, holding out the glowing orb. "This represents the Springbok in the sky," he said, his voice ringing with newfound authority. "By disrespecting the animal, you disrespect the stars themselves."

The hunters exchanged nervous glances. The sight of the glowing orb and the conviction in Keletso's voice seemed to shake their bravado.

Sensing their hesitation, Keletso pressed on. "We hunt to survive, not for greed. Take only what you need and leave an offering for the life force you take."

A tense silence hung in the air. Finally, the leader of the other hunters dipped his head in a grudging acknowledgement. "We will hunt elsewhere," he muttered, his voice filled with a hint of shame. With that, the hunters loaded the springbok onto their steeds and rode away.

Mxolisi placed a hand on Keletso's shoulder, a smile on his face. "You have done well," he said, his voice stronger than it had been in weeks. "You have become a guardian of the land, a bridge between the past and the future."

News of Keletso's encounter with the Star Chasers and his stand against the disrespectful hunters spread like wildfire through the Kalahari. He became a symbol of the San people's reawakening connection to their celestial heritage.

Keletso and Mxolisi, along with other elders, began teaching the younger generations the old ways – tracking by the stars, understanding constellations, and respecting the delicate balance of the ecosystem. They formed a council, "The Keepers of the Stars," dedicated to preserving the San traditions and ensuring a future where humans lived in harmony with the land and the cosmos.

Years passed. Mxolisi, though frail, lived much longer than expected, his spirit revitalized by the night of the Star Chasers. Keletso, a respected leader among his people, continued his grandfather's legacy.

One night, under the same vast canvas of stars, Keletso stood beside a group of young children, pointing to the Milky Way. He told them the stories of the San, the celestial creatures, and the Star Chasers. He spoke of the importance of respecting the land and the night sky, the source of wisdom and wonder.

As he spoke, a faint blue light streaked across the sky, a silent testament to the Star Chasers' continued journey. Keletso smiled, knowing that the connection between his people and the cosmos would live on, carried by the stars and the stories whispered under the night sky.

THE FIRE OF KNOWLEDGE

Based on the African legend
about the Origin of Fire.

This Xhosa story tells of a bird named Nkaita, who originally guarded the secret of fire. After a sequence of events, the benevolent Mantis finally succeeded in stealing fire from Nkaita and gave it to the people. The story illustrates the importance of fire in daily life and the human desire for knowledge.

Nkaita stared out the window of her cramped apartment; the city lights a glittering counterpoint to the inky sky. Her dark eyes, the same shade as the raven she was named after, held a deep well of loneliness. Unlike the mythical Nkaita of Xhosa legend, guardian of fire, this Nkaita guarded something else: knowledge.

Nkaita wasn't a literal bird but a prodigy. She'd skipped grades, leaving her classmates behind like fallen feathers. Now, at 16, she was already enrolled in a prestigious university program, a scholarship student surrounded by privilege she couldn't relate to. Knowledge, for her, had been the fire, the only warmth in a life devoid of family.

One day, a new professor arrived, Dr Malik. His eyes, like embers, held a spark that ignited something in Nkaita. He saw the fire within her, the thirst for knowledge that mirrored his own. Unlike her other teachers, who treated her brilliance with detached respect, Dr Malik fanned the flames.

He invited her to his office, a haven of ancient books and scientific equipment. Here, Nkaita wasn't just a prodigy; she was a colleague. Dr Malik shared his research on forgotten knowledge and hidden connections between ancient myths and modern science. It was exhilarating, a feast for her hungry mind.

But Dr Malik's warmth was short-lived. He became secretive, spending long nights locked in his office. Nkaita, consumed by a newfound curiosity, peeked in one evening. She saw him hunched over a dusty artefact, its surface shimmering with an unnatural light.

Dr Malik caught her. Panic flickered in his eyes,

replaced by a desperate plea. "Nkaita," he said, "this knowledge can be dangerous in the wrong hands. Promise me you won't tell anyone."

Nkaita was torn. The loyalty she felt for Dr Malik warred with her desire to understand. Was this the fire he'd been guarding, a metaphorical one of forbidden knowledge?

Memories of the Xhosa legend surfaced – Nkaita, the bird, hoarding knowledge like fire. Was she making the same mistake?

Days turned into weeks, and the weight of the secret began to wear on Nkaita. Dr Malik, paranoid and withdrawn, pushed her away. Finally, Nkaita realized she had a choice: become a hoarder of knowledge like the mythical bird or share it like the benevolent Mantis who brought fire to humanity.

Hesitantly, Nkaita went to the university administration, revealing Dr Malik's secret research and the artefact's strange power. It was a difficult decision, but the fire of knowledge, she realized, needed to be shared, its power harnessed for the greater good.

Dr Malik was investigated and suspended for his reckless research. But Nkaita, once isolated, became a beacon. Her bravery sparked the interest of other professors, who recognized her talent and thirst for knowledge. She still cherished her solitude, but now it was tempered with a sense of belonging.

The experience changed Nkaita. She finally understood the lesson of fire, both literal and metaphorical. Knowledge, like fire, was a powerful tool, but it had to be wielded responsibly and shared generously for the benefit of all. Nkaita, the solitary bird, was learning to soar with the flock, her fire illuminating the path ahead.

THE TORTOISE

Based on the African legend of the Talking Tortoise.

The Talking Tortoise is a character found in many African folktales, including South African versions. In one story, the Tortoise tricks the birds into teaching him how to fly, leading to amusing and clever outcomes.

Trevor "Tortoise" Thornton wasn't your average high schooler. While his classmates slaved over homework and fretted over university applications, Trevor spent his days scheming. Not for good grades, mind you, but for the ultimate high: pranking unsuspecting primary schoolers.

Trevor's chosen weapon? His voice. Unlike the legendary talking tortoise, Trevor couldn't actually make his own voice change. But he was a master of impressions, able to mimic teachers, parents, and even cartoon characters with uncanny accuracy.

His current target was little Timmy, a wide-eyed first grader with a backpack bigger than himself. Trevor spotted Timmy clutching a prized Pokémon card, a holographic Charizard. A mischievous glint flickered in Trevor's eyes.

He cleared his throat, making his voice sound gruff and authoritative. "Timmy," he boomed, mimicking Principal Jones' sternest tone. "Detention! The library needs your help sorting ancient scrolls … immediately."

Timmy's eyes widened. Detention? In first grade? He glanced nervously at the closed library door, his imagination conjuring images of dusty scrolls and hungry librarians. Sniffling back tears, he clutched his Charizard card tighter and scurried into the library.

Trevor doubled over, his laughter echoing down the empty hallway. He'd pulled it off again. But the thrill was short-lived. Later that day, a frantic Mrs. Ramirez, Timmy's mother, stormed into the principal's office.

"My Timmy is traumatized!" she shrieked, waving a crumpled note. "He says Principal Jones sent him to detention for scrolls?"

Principal Jones, a man with the patience of a

saint, sputtered in disbelief. "Detention? Scrolls? Nonsense!"

The gravity of the situation finally hit Trevor. He hadn't anticipated Timmy's blind obedience, his fear of authority. Guilt gnawed at him as Principal Jones delivered a scathing lecture about the importance of trust and responsibility.

The next day, Trevor, head hung low, approached Timmy in the playground. Timmy, still traumatized, shrank back. Trevor, his voice gruff with remorse, confessed to the prank, mimicking his own voice this time.

Timmy, bewildered, stared at him with tear-filled eyes. "You mean it wasn't Principal Jones?"

Trevor nodded, shamefaced. Timmy looked at his prized Charizard card, its once-vibrant colours now tinged with the memory of fake detention. He shoved it back in his pocket, a silent accusation.

The prank, once hilarious, now felt hollow. Trevor realized the talking tortoise was a trickster but a clever one. He'd fooled the birds, not terrorized them. Trevor, the modern talking tortoise, hadn't just landed a prank – he'd crushed a child's trust.

News of the incident spread like wildfire. Trevor, once a prankster extraordinaire, became "Tortured Tortoise," a cautionary tale. He swore off his voice-mimicking antics, his days now filled with genuine attempts to make amends. Maybe, just maybe, unlike the legendary tortoise who flew with borrowed wings, Trevor, with a little hard work, could earn some real trust, his own voice finally leading the way.

THE THIEF

Based on the African story about
The White Elephant.

In this folktale, a hunter encounters a
mysterious White Elephant that transforms
into a beautiful girl. She marries the hunter but
warns him never to tell anyone about her true
form. When he shares the secret, she returns
to her elephant state and disappears, leaving
a valuable lesson about trust and loyalty.

Aïsha wasn't your average data analyst. Her past life as a top-tier hacker remained a tightly coded secret, a ghost in the machine she desperately wished to erase. Years ago, she craved a quiet life offline after a daring digital heist for a notorious syndicate. Legend spoke of a secluded server farm in the Namib desert guarded by a renowned digital nomad called the "Cloud Weaver." Aïsha, fuelled by a yearning for normalcy, ventured into the harsh desert landscape. She typed her wish on a dusty keyboard inside the server farm, and the room hummed with energy. When the silence returned, the intricate network of code on her screen transformed into rows of bread recipes. Aïsha was free to start a new life.

Years later, with the faint scent of fresh bread clinging to her skin, she met Kwesi, a kind-hearted baker with a warm smile. He was drawn to her quiet intelligence, oblivious to the digital shadows she kept hidden. Love blossomed, and they married under a canopy of fairy lights in their cosy bakery. Still burdened by guilt, Aïsha confessed her past to Kwesi, begging him to keep it a secret.He promised, his eyes reflecting sincerity through his digital glasses.

Aïsha thrived in her new life. But Kwesi, plagued by insecurities about his own modest background, felt overshadowed by Aïsha's past exploits. One evening, after indulging in a virtual reality game a little too intensely, he found himself confiding in his online friend 'The Ghost' about Aïsha's secret. Like a mischievous virus, the news quickly spread through the virtual realm, reaching Aïsha's formidable mother-in-law, Mama Akua. Coincidentally, Mama Akua's prized digital artwork collection vanished that night.

Accusations flew like coded messages across encrypted channels. Aïsha, her heart cracking with betrayal, pleaded her innocence. The stolen artwork remained missing, and a cold suspicion settled over their once-warm bakery. Kwesi, drowning in digital regret, tried to repair the fractured firewalls of their trust, but the damage was done. Aïsha, unable to bear the suffocating atmosphere, disconnected from their shared life.

Alone and ostracised by her in-law family, tears blurring her vision through her tear-resistant goggles, Aïsha understood the true weight of Kwesi's broken promise. Years later, a real hacker was apprehended, and the stolen artwork was recovered. Aïsha, though relieved, carried the scars of Kwesi's betrayal. Working from a hidden corner of the web, she started a network called "The Offline Haven," helping others ostracized by society for digital sins. In beginning this network, she discovered a strength she never knew she possessed.

This painful experience became her guiding code. Trust, she realized, was the encryption that secured relationships. Without it, love became corrupted, suspicion became malware, and even the strongest bonds crumbled. Though scarred, Aïsha emerged stronger, forever marked by the vital lesson: trust, nurtured and protected, is the firewall upon which love truly thrives.

While monitoring the network traffic one evening,

a familiar digital signature appeared - The Ghost. Guilt crackled through the message, a desperate plea for forgiveness. Kwesi, having learned a harsh lesson, had taken on the mantle of a "Digital Guardian," using his skills to protect vulnerable networks.

Aïsha smiled, a flicker of warmth bridging the digital divide. Maybe, just maybe, there was a chance to rewrite their code, to rebuild trust, one byte at a time. The scars may remain, but within the vast digital landscape, a glimmer of hope flickered, a testament to the enduring power of forgiveness and the transformative strength of trust.

A tense silence hung in the virtual air as Aïsha stared at The Ghost's message. Memories, both sweet and bitter, flooded her mind. Kwesi's warm smile, the joy of creating bread together, and the sting of betrayal flickered across her digital vision like a corrupted video feed.

Taking a deep breath, Aïsha typed a response. It was short, just a simple question: "Do you truly believe in a second chance?"

The reply came almost instantly. "More than

anything," it read, followed by a string of repentant emojis. Aïsha knew words wouldn't erase the past; trust, like a cracked firewall, wouldn't be easily repaired. But Kwesi's actions spoke louder than his digital pleas. His work as a "Digital Guardian" was a testament to his remorse and desire to make amends.

A plan began to form in Aïsha's mind. "There's a vulnerable network of schools in a remote village," she typed, "They lack the resources to protect themselves from malware and digital scams. It's a high-risk mission, but it could be a good start."

"I'm in," came the immediate reply.

The mission was far from easy. The remote village, nestled deep in the heart of the savanna, had limited internet access, making communication a challenge. Kwesi was used to the fast-paced world of online gaming and had to adapt to the villagers' slower, more deliberate pace. Aïsha, on the other hand, used her baking skills to build relationships with the community. Sharing fresh bread while teaching them about cybersecurity was a winning formula.

Over the weeks, slowly, brick by digital brick, trust began to rebuild between Aïsha and Kwesi and the villagers and the digital world. With his newfound passion for protecting vulnerable networks, Kwesi earned the villagers' respect. Aïsha, seeing Kwesi's dedication, began to forgive, the bitterness replaced by a cautious hope.

One evening, as they sat by a crackling bonfire beneath a star-studded sky, the villagers presented them with a gift – a carved wooden elephant, its surface smooth and intricate. Kwesi, a mischievous grin on his face, nudged Aïsha. "Looks familiar, doesn't it?" he whispered.

Aïsha smiled, a memory surfacing. Years ago, when she'd first entered the server farm, she'd come across a dusty legend – of a powerful program called "The White Elephant," an entity that granted wishes but demanded absolute trust. Back then, she'd scoffed at the fable. Now, holding the intricately carved elephant, she understood. The White Elephant wasn't a program; it was a metaphor. Trust, like the delicate tusks of the elephant, needed to be protected and cared for. Like a cracked tusk, a broken promise could shatter the very bond it was meant to strengthen.

As they sat by the fire, Aïsha knew their journey was far from over. There would be more challenges and more digital threats to overcome. But now, they had a foundation – a shared purpose, a renewed trust in each other, and a village they had sworn to protect. The stars above twinkled, a silent testament to their second chance, a chance born from betrayal, forgiveness, and the enduring strength of trust.

ABOUT THE AUTHOR

Lisa Bell

I have been writing romantic fiction since a teen, and what started as a way to escape, has now materialised into a passion and love. Whilst running my digital marketing agency, I still somehow manage to  escape into my fantasy world of words whenever I get a gap.
I would describe my style of writing as easy-go-to-fantasy.

My go-to genre is young adult urban fantasy, however, I am venturing in unknowns since turning 50, and I am excited to see what my imagination can produce.

BOOKS BY THIS AUTHOR

Travellers

What would you do if you found out that you had been lied to from birth? That you had been brought up with protection in mind? That you are capable of amazing magical things … but that your parents had ensured they you never found out?

Rebecca finds this out from a complete stranger. Mysterious Ben literally sweeps her away into a world of magic, danger, and downright craziness.

She is thrown into a whirlwind dystopia where she needs to hone her newly-found powers with no time to spare and discovers that she has more to offer than she thought.

Together they embark on an action-packed race to save themselves and their kind.

Travellers is Book 1 in the Centurion Duet.

Seekers

Book 2 in the Centurion Duet - The adventure and madness continue as Rebecca and Ben's relationship is challenged by a ghost from the past. The Seekers reveal a secret that may threaten to destroy them all. And Rebecca must step up to her Centurion status before their race is lost forever.

Don't Wake Up

Love is blind ... or so they say ... but what if you're not sure you even exist? We take a poignant and sweet journey with our two young protagonists as they explore a new fantastical world and first love.

GET IN TOUCH WITH THE AUTHOR

I would love to hear from you ...

Website - https://lisabell.co.za/

Social Accounts:

Facebook - https://www.facebook.com/lisabellauthor

Instagram - https://www.instagram.com/lisabellauthor/